Praise for the Night Stalkers series:

Two Titles in
"Best 101 Romance Novels of the Last 10 years"
– Booklist

"Top 10 Romance of 2012."
– Booklist, *The Night Is Mine*

"Top 5 Romance of 2012."
–NPR, *I Own the Dawn*

"Suzanne Brockmann fans will love this."
–Booklist, *Wait Until Dark*

"Best 5 Romance of 2013."
–Barnes & Noble, *Take Over at Midnight*

"Nominee for Reviewer's Choice Award
for Best Romantic Suspense of 2014."
–RT Book Reviews, *Light Up the Night*

"Score 5 – Reviewer Top Pick – Buchman writes
with unusual sensitivity and delicacy for such a
hard-edged genre."
–Publishers Weekly, *Bring On the Dusk*

The Night Stalkers

Zachary's Christmas

by

M. L. Buchman

Discover more by this author at:
www.mlbuchman.com

Cover images:
Man Giving Fresh Flowers To Woman Photo
© Andreypopov | Dreamstime.com
A young and sexy brunette woman on a foggy background
© Maksim Shmeljov | Dreamstime.com
USAF C-32A © Sam Meyer | Wikimedia Commons
Red and Green Candy cane over white
© Lucie Lang | Dreamstime.com (back cover)

Buchman Bookworks

Other works by M. L. Buchman:

The Night Stalkers
The Night Is Mine
I Own the Dawn
Daniel's Christmas
Wait Until Dark
Frank's Independence Day
Peter's Christmas
Take Over at Midnight
Light Up the Night
Christmas at Steel Beach
Bring On the Dusk
Target of the Heart
Target Lock on Love
Christmas at Peleliu Cove
Zachary's Christmas

Firehawks
Pure Heat
Wildfire at Dawn
Full Blaze
Wildfire at Larch Creek
Wildfire on the Skagit
Hot Point

Delta Force
Target Engaged

Angelo's Hearth
Where Dreams are Born
Where Dreams Reside
Maria's Christmas Table
Where Dreams Unfold
Where Dreams Are Written

Dieties Anonymous
Cookbook from Hell: Reheated
Saviors 101

Thrillers
Swap Out!
One Chef!
Two Chef!

SF/F Titles
Nara
Monk's Maze

Chapter 1

Brother, is it ever tricky to break into this place," Melanie Anne Darlington plummeted into her sibling's office chair. Then she had to scrape her hair out of her face; long hair and a thick parka complete with a furred collar and hood kept trapping her behind a blond curtain. She'd never been good at being a woman of mystery.

Daniel would know of course, that his big sister was dropping in for an unannounced visit since the moment she'd hit the outermost layer of White House security. Not quite like the old days when she could drop unexpectedly out of the hayloft and scare the daylights out of him—a joke that simply never grew old—but there was still satisfaction to be had. And she'd come accompanied by her own personal White House guard—looking very spiffy in his blue uniform and white hat—just in case he didn't welcome the "surprise."

"Hey, Sister. Where's your rifle, Anne? I assume you're hunting polar bear in that outfit." His lazy Tennessee accent was more diluted by Washington DC every time she saw him and it made her feel even more alone than she already did, which at the moment was saying more than a thing or two. But his smile was warm as always and that helped some.

"You will *not* be insulting my parka. It's never seventeen degrees on December first! Don't you gentlemen pass laws and sign bills against precisely this kind of travesty?" The city was cloaked in ice and a recent snow.

It had looked magical from the airplane and the cab, with all the landmark buildings popping up out of the vast whiteness as if they themselves were formed of snow. And signs of Christmas had been everywhere, from a tiny wreath above baggage claim to giant fake candy canes on street lamps to the massive National Christmas Tree on The Ellipse.

Once afoot though, the cold had cut right to the bone. But if Daniel thought he'd be getting away with insulting her attire, he had another think coming.

Of course Mister Cover-of-*GQ*—the blond boy-genius turned White House Chief of Staff by the age of thirty—would never think of wearing a parka. His corner office glowed a warm orange with the setting sun. Her own little brother had a southwest-facing corner office in the West Wing—that was completely crazy. The only sign of Christmas from here was a massive wreath on the Eisenhower Executive Office Building across the street. The White House hadn't been decorated yet.

"I'll have them draft special legislation just for you. Would you prefer a military escort with portable heaters?"

"Now that be sweet of you," the Tennesseans' way of calling someone a jerk in public, "though maybe if you selected a few particularly hunky ones, that would have some nice possibilities." She slapped her hand against her coat's thick padding, "If the apocalypse hits tomorrow, this is going to be far more practical than one of your three-piece suits and designer-Ralph wool coats, City Boy. Besides, how am I supposed to hunt a decent bear, even a stuffed one for Christmas, when they've confiscated my popgun at the front gate." She waved a hand at the guard who had escorted her through the last leg of her journey. "Do you think the spiffy soldier will lend me his sword if I bat my eyelashes?"

"He's not a soldier, he's a Marine, and I think he'd be crazy if he did." Daniel looked up at the man in question. "We're fine here, Jeffrey; you'll want to escape while you still can. She's a man eater."

The Marine saluted and, in a flash of humor that she suspected was rare for a White House honor guardsman said, "Thank you for the warning, sir." He did a neat turn on his heel and marched back out into the hall to his post outside the Oval Office, his boot heels sounding smartly against the hardwood flooring.

"Am not a man eater."

"Are too."

"Am not," she looked up over his shoulder, "am I Mr. President?"

Daniel startled to his feet and she belatedly rose to her own as Peter Matthews strode in through the side door of Daniel's office. The President was a tall, handsome man with dark hair and lively eyes that always made him look even kinder than he already was.

"Hello, Anne. You been out moose hunting?" He came around to offer her a friendly handshake. He earned additional points for recalling that she went by her middle name.

"Sir, between you and my brother you are two of the handsomest ex-bachelors around, but you share the same lousy sense of humor. I'll talk to your wife about fixing that for you."

"Trust me, Genny has tried," the President dropped into the other chair and she and Daniel resumed their own. It still startled her every time he did something like that; Peter Matthews always had time to be pleasant.

"If you two have something to talk about, I can go upstairs and see you later." But the President was patting his hand in the air for her to stay in place.

"Nothing that won't keep. How's the farm?"

"It's…" She was finally warm enough to unzip her coat. Toying with the zip gave her a moment to steel herself before confronting Daniel. It was what she'd come to DC to talk to him about. Gently. After testing the waters very carefully. Daniel had always been crazy about the family farm. By some strange chance, that was what had led him to DC and the White House. Even here in the Chief of Staff's office—when the historical decorators offered him a selection from the greatest works of art—he'd put up four big panoramas of their family farm, one in each season.

The rest of the furniture was ornate, classic, probably from some period of history they'd tried to teach her about in high school when she couldn't care less. Memorize the facts, spit them out, get the A, forget them. The only incongruous part of her brother's office was his desk. The piece itself was a majestic piece of cherrywood, but a battle raged upon what little showed of its surface with no victor yet proclaimed. File folders in a rainbow of coded colors teetered against other stacks of plain manila. Thick-bound volumes bore official looking report titles that were gleefully driving the lone computer monitor inch by grudging inch toward its doom off the edge of the desk.

The only reason that she could tell it was cherrywood rather than battered old plywood was a small, carefully walled off corner that contained only two objects. A beautiful Advent calendar with only its first door opened stood stout guard over the wedding picture of her brother and Alice now-Darlington III—the coolest sister-in-law on the planet. A top CIA analyst, she was even smarter than Anne's brilliant brother. Their wedding on the farm had been…

The farm.

Sighing that things never seemed to go quite the way she intended, she turned to face the President.

"The farm sucks, Mr. President." She could see Daniel jolt upright out of the corner of her eye so she turned to face the problem head on. "The farm is jes' fine, baby brother. So relax yourself some. It's only me who is going madder than a hatter.

You were built for that place; I wasn't. The foreman, the manager, Ma and Pop, the streaming hordes just begging to work at the cuisine training center on the model Slow Food farm of the entire Southeastern US—none of them need me there."

"But you did all of the Thanksgiving events and it was amazing."

"Thanks. And I'd rather shoot myself with a popgun than go through it again." She'd done the grand hostess gig for the Darlington Thanksgiving—the fanciest affair on the farm's annual event calendar. Dinner for hundreds, not a Tennessee Congressman who hadn't been invited along with his family. She'd made sure that *Food and Wine* as well as the key food bloggers had not only received the recipes, but invitations to the banquet as well. It had been a grand affair and Anne had been at the center of it. That was one of the things that had driven her to escape the farm now, Ma and Pop had been pushing her to take on the estate's entire event division and she'd…run away. Real mature, but there was not a chance that she'd be telling her little brother that.

"I'm bored shitless," which was also true. She could do these big events in her sleep now, and she couldn't imagine feeling less excited about anything.

Daniel flinched at her language.

Maybe she had gone a little too far considering the company. She turned slowly to face the President. "Sorry sir. You may not know this, but I was raised on a farm. I speak that way far too often for Daniel's liking. I failed my kindergarten training to be a polite Southern lady and never recovered."

"A farm, really?" He offered in mock surprise. "I grew up in DC. I'll trash talk with you any day you want."

She knew from various visits over the last three years since Daniel rose to Chief of Staff that Peter Matthews could barely say "darn" without blushing and her brother wasn't all that much better.

"You're on, sir. Some night we'll each have a beer, which is about my limit anyway, and we'll choose a topic. Maybe you," she pointed at her brother. "We'll make him attend but won't let him speak. I'll tell you childhood horror stories, like the first time he kissed a girl—she was six and he was seven, the mad womanizer—I'm the one who caught them."

"And you haven't let me live down Becky Carpenter yet."

"Hush now. I'm not talking to you, I'm talking to the President," she kept her attention on Peter Matthews. "You can tell me Washington stories. I still don't understand how my dirt-loving brother ended up at the center of power and I ended up at the center of whole passel of dirt."

"Just lucky I guess," Daniel growled. "I'd trade this in a heartbeat, if—" He bit his tongue.

It was an interesting moment. The President had gone very still. Anne considered gunning for Daniel while he was down but decided that was too cruel despite her big-sisterly responsibilities to harass him whenever possible.

"If what, Daniel?" The President's tone had gone soft and difficult to read. "I wouldn't be the first President to run through two Chiefs of Staff. Do you want out?"

"No, sir," he immediately replied. No doubt, no equivocation. Her brother had grown a real spine while she wasn't watching— which only made her feel all the more lost. Like an elf kicked out of the Christmas workshop for painting candy canes pink and black, but who had nowhere else to go because Santa's workshop was indeed at the North Pole.

"If what, Daniel?"

"It's an honor to serve and—"

"He did grow up on a farm, didn't he?" The President turned to her, interrupting Daniel. "I'm from DC but I know when someone heaves a shovel of horse crap at me."

"*That* was horseshit, Mr. President. And yes sir, my brother is slinging it." She turned back to Daniel, "Maybe I should become Chief of Staff and you should return to the farm. Neither of us is where we want to be."

"Give it to me straight, Daniel," the President spoke in his this-bill-will-pass tone that was so effective on national TV.

Daniel dug his hands through his hair, actually mussing it up. Anne was sorry she'd trapped him enough to make him feel that way, but she didn't know how to take it back in the current situation.

"We're doing so much good here, Peter," Daniel had dropped the honorific, which she could see surprised the President more than anything that had come before. Then Daniel did finally blush. "Sorry, Mr. President. I came to DC to help jumpstart the Slow Food movement, farm-to-table. I came to promote fresh, unprocessed ingredients that are farmed rather than GMO agri-business. I had never imagined what I've ended up doing here. It's amazing and I love it!" He started picking up folders off his desk. "The next G-20 meeting. The Southeast Asia trading pact. Watershed restoration. I wouldn't want to miss a single day of it."

"But you miss the farm that," the President turned to her, "your sister hates."

"I do, Mr. President," they said in unison with exactly the same intonation.

# # #

Zachary Thomas typically went directly from his office to the Oval Office when visiting the White House. President Peter Matthews had made it clear that his Vice President was to be barred from no meeting and was always welcome there. VPs had so often—and occasionally notoriously—been kept out of the loop, that even after five years Zack couldn't get used to the privilege. There were VPs who had never once used their office just next door to the Chief of Staff's. The bulk of his own staff worked across the street in the Eisenhower Executive Office Building, but he was in the West Wing at least a portion of every day.

He heard the President's laugh from Daniel's office, so he turned in rather than continuing down to the Oval. Janet offered her typical teasing smile—that of a woman on the verge of retirement who had offered more than once to run off to Tangiers with him—and waved him through.

"If only I were a few decades older, and we were both unwed," he told her. Janet had aged very well, but he'd met her very attentive husband.

"We need to be finding you a wife, Mr. Vice President. Or I will leave poor James for you."

"I just might take you up on that, ma'am. Best warn him to start looking." They traded winks then Zack strode up to the threshold.

Peter Matthews was the first President since Polk in the mid-1800s who wore his dark hair casually long—LBJ's gray coif had only appeared after his retirement. It made Peter look boyish and handsome, aided by being the youngest President ever elected. The gray that came with the office was only beginning to show. Daniel, his Chief of Staff, wore his blond hair short, but he had that California surfer-boy handsomeness despite his Tennessee farm heritage. Neither had the military bearing of having served, though it was hard to fault the choices the President had made over the years.

Zack was more of a tall Colorado boy—Colorado Springs born-and-buttered. It was a distinction little understood outside the state and one used carefully inside the state. His hometown had shrugged off almost all of its early counter-culture roots except in small outlier enclaves like Manitou Springs. Now it was known for one of three things: the US Olympic Training Center, the Air Force Academy, and headquarters for over fifty Evangelical churches. When spoken in-state, Zack only had to add one word, "I'm from The Springs...Academy." That was a whole conversation had, and answered. Out-of-state, he just said "Colorado" without even mentioning the city's name. It was easier that way.

Daniel sat as respectfully as always, perhaps sitting so carefully upright in order to be seen across the prairie-sized expanse of paperwork he called a desk. The President remained in his chair, looking more relaxed than Daniel, but proper as always.

Beside him, in profile, sat a woman with a beauty as surprising as Daniel's. They were obviously related, so this must be the sister he'd heard tales of but never met. Melanie Anne Darlington. Daniel's rugged handsomeness had been translated into her fine features; his short blond hair transformed into a sun-streaked cascade that spilled down over the furred collar of her oversized parka.

The mood in the room was an odd mixture. Daniel was confused and perhaps angry. The President and Daniel's sister were both laughing, hers a bright spill on the air.

"Hello, Mr. Vice President," Daniel spotted him and rose, just as he would for the President. It was always a kind compliment that his predecessor had certainly never offered…before he'd been hauled off for treason on other matters.

The President glanced over, "Hello, Zack."

The woman turned and the full impact of her sparkling eyes, the darkest blue he'd ever seen, almost had him stepping backwards. Behind those beautiful features was clearly a very sharp mind. And her beauty while not of some fantastical portion, was all the stronger for the woman who lived behind them; she was vibrant. A massive parka hung open from her shoulders, but the bulk made it difficult to assess her figure.

"Where do I sign up?"

She looked up at him in surprise. She too had risen along with her brother but it was a fair way from his own six-two down to her five-foot-six.

"For the polar expedition that you're obviously leading," he clarified.

"Have to bring your own parka," her smile went from tentative to radiant.

"Done," he offered a hand and she shook it firmly. Fine fingers had nothing to do with this woman's obvious strength. "Zachary Thomas. But expedition leaders can call me Zack."

"Thank you, Mr. Vice President. I'll remember that. Anne Darlington, expedition leader." Then she turned back to the President. "See? At least one man in this administration has a decent sense of humor."

"Only happens around beautiful women,"—which she was and more. She had a much stronger accent than her brother, unmistakably Tennessee. Like a blond and slightly taller Holly Hunter who he'd always had a weak spot for in the movies. "You sound just like—"

"Don't you be doing that," she cut him off and shook a finger at him. "I do *not* sound like her. Not if you want to stay on my expedition. Besides, she's from Georgia. That's a whole different place," she pronounced 'whole' as if it had three or four Ls, exactly as Holly Hunter would have.

"Yes, ma'am," he saluted her sharply. Zack looked to Peter Matthews, "Should I come back later?" The tension still rippled about the room. Though no one had ever accused him of having a sense of humor before, she made him want to try. "In the meantime, if the lady would like, I can go out and rustle up a dog team with sled. That might prove difficult in Washington DC, but I'm willing to give it a go."

Again that laugh spilled forth so easily and brightened the room still further. Then she turned to her brother.

"Okay, Daniel, I'll make you a deal. One time offer, but you must decide right away. I'll go back to the farm, but only if I can take my team with me," she stepped over and hooked a hand about Zack's elbow to demonstrate their solidarity.

"I'm sorry, but you can't have him," Peter Matthews shook his head. "Zack still has a job here."

"With all due respect, Mr. President…Tough!"

Zack didn't even try to stop the laugh that come out of him as she faced down the President of the United States.

"This man here," she lifted Zack's elbow as if she needed to clarify which one, "applied, was accepted, and signed the ship's articles. He's mine now. Besides, I like his smile."

And when she smiled up at him, he couldn't help but return it.

"Hate to correct you, Ma'am. Truly I do," Zack should be backing away, this was Daniel's sister, but he was enjoying the little scene and the way her hand felt on his arm. "However, there are no ship's articles as I'm retired Air Force, not Navy. And I regret to inform you that I did swear before the nation to uphold this Vice Presidential office as well as several other odds and ends. Like, oh, the Constitution."

"Traitor!" She let go of his arm, clasped her hands over her heart, before collapsing back into her chair as if struck down. "I've been betrayed. I suppose you may have him back, Mr. President. I wouldn't trust him though. Far too honorable. Unlike me."

The President waved Zack to a seat. The only open one was close beside Ms. Darlington, which was just fine with him.

"So, what are we debating?"

"Whether or not Daniel and I should trade jobs. What do you think?"

He could only assume she was joking, but there was something in the President's look that made him less than certain. Normally that would cause Zack to approach such a question with caution and diplomacy. But with Anne Darlington sitting beside him…

Clambering back out of his chair, he grabbed Anne's wrist, dragged her to her feet, and tugged her around the desk after him.

She giggled, which was awfully cute on her. So he went with it.

"Out, Daniel. Out!" Zack shooed him away.

Daniel remained paralyzed for a second, then, puzzled, scrambled to his feet.

Zack bowed toward the woman as if she wore an evening gown rather than a heavy parka, jeans, and craftsman-stitched custom-made cowboy boots which said just as much as a designer gown would have about who she was. The Darlingtons weren't just Tennessee farmers; they were one of the power families of the South.

"My lady leader, your chair awaits."

# # #

Anne curtsied, holding out the hem of her parka, before sitting regally in the seat as if on a throne.

She looked up at the three men.

Vice President Zachary Thomas utterly charming and terribly handsome in his role of momentarily playing the jester. He was tall, dark-haired, and wore one of those close beards that he kept at just a week's length. On his strong face, it looked mature and thoughtful rather than unkempt as most such beards did. She'd never much fancied a man in a beard, but the Vice President perhaps could convince her otherwise. His military background was easily seen in perfect posture, an inordinate strength for a politician, and a degree of self-assuredness that few men had.

The President still sat with an unreadable half smile on his face.

And Daniel remained on his feet, looking actively distressed.

Then she looked at the desk in front of her and began reading report titles: *Antarctic Climate Change Update. Southeast Asia—an analysis of potential armed conflict over China's latest Spratly Island militarization. Terrorist activity in…*

A bit overwhelmed, she looked up again.

The President of the United States still sat directly across the desk and was watching her with a carefully neutral expression. As if in some alternate reality he'd consider it if both she and Daniel said yes. There was an unnerving thought.

She'd never really appreciated what Daniel did before. He sorted, filtered, prioritized all this information into a form digestible by the man sitting across from her. It didn't look hard from the other side of the desk—but from here it looked impossible. And the responsibility of it was overwhelming.

Her kid brother stood there, shifting from foot to foot, a nervous habit he'd had since he was a little boy.

"When did you change so much?" It was barely a whisper, but it was all she could manage.

Daniel shrugged uneasily, as if uncertain what she meant. Maybe he didn't know how different he'd become; she almost didn't recognize him. The fine suit was the least of it. The beautiful and brilliant wife, the amazing job, finding a place he belonged in the nation's capital—in the heart of it. Taken altogether it was an alarming change.

Only that trademark shifting of feet—which she suspected only happened now in his big sister's presence—still identified him as the boy she'd known since birth. He was her very first memory. She'd been three on the day her brother had come home and squalled right in her face—the moment before burping up all over her. It was a day she had yet to let him off the hook for.

Well, she knew one thing about him in the here and now for certain. Anne rose to her feet. "*You* belong here. Right here." She swiveled the chair partly in his direction and moved away.

She shoved her hands in her pockets and pulled the parka tightly about her. A chill shivered through her and it was all she could do to hide it.

Yet another place she *didn't* belong.

"I'll just go up to the Residence. See you later, Daniel. Mr. President and Mr. Vice President."

She slipped out of the office, past Daniel's secretary, and wished she could pull up the parka's hood. Would have, if it wouldn't make every single Marine and Secret Service agent stop her as she crossed from the West Wing to the Residence.

She passed through hordes of Christmas decorators, all escorted by multitudes of Secret Service agents. The White House was transforming around her, but still she remained the same. She wished they could redecorate her so easily.

Anne plowed through and—more by luck than thought— found her way out of the West Wing and over to the Residence. For the first time in decades the Chief of Staff lived in the White House—the President had given Daniel use of the third floor. It was a holdover from the year when both Peter and Daniel had been bachelors.

Now the President, his wife Geneviève Matthews, and their little girl Adele lived on the second floor. Daniel lived on the third with his wife Alice.

And she lived…in a parka while wandering through the long halls of the White House. A few people eyed her curiously, but she made it to the elevator and up to the third floor without being stopped. At least that one thing had gone well today.

Chapter 2

A*fter their meeting was* done, Zack Thomas swung through his office to gather his coat. He took the stairs down to the West Wing lobby. Clutters of rushing staffers dodged aside to open a passage for him. Heading up the stairs, the Communications Director passed him, in a deep debate with one of the speechwriters, offering a quick nod without breaking stride.

It was decorating day and while the West Wing didn't get the level of treatment accorded to the Residence, a stream of volunteers did what they could to remain out of the way while totting mantel swags, holly boughs, and curiously two of them carrying a child mannequin in a Victorian-era Christmas outfit.

"Please tell me that isn't headed for my office."

The young woman holding the mannequin's shoulders mumbled something about that being up to the West Wing Director of Decorations and moved on without recognizing him.

Zack seriously hoped that the Victorian motif was whimsical or even ironic rather than thematic to this year's decoration plan.

He finally reached the lobby, which the decorators had yet to reach and the congestion eased to normal levels of West Wing mayhem. With her impeccable timing, that he could only credit to her having him wired with a geo-locator when he wasn't watching, his assistant appeared from the opposite side of the lobby. She was dressed in one of her understated wool knee-length designer coats that looked so good on her tall, slender frame; the red wool a tasteful contrast to the dark brunette swing of hair that brushed her collar. She moved like an elegant VP-seeking missile through the heart of the crowd and they all stepped aside for her.

Cornelia Day held his coat's collar for him as he shrugged into it.

"What else do I have today? Anything pressing?"

She retained his entire schedule in her head, just one of her many daunting skills. "Surround yourself with people smarter than you," was the one rare piece of advice from his father-the-two-star-General. Cornelia was definitely one of those people. She'd served him since she'd interned for him as the Governor of Colorado, straight out of Claremont McKenna College—graduated at nineteen with full honors. He'd moved her to his full-time assistant four weeks later and six months after that he wondered how he'd ever survived without her.

"End of day wrap up with me. Not even a dinner meeting," she buttoned her coat as if the EEOB offices were far more than a hundred feet from the West Wing. Cornelia often complained about having to move from Southern California to Colorado to work for him. But her time there had prepared her wardrobe for the current Washington, DC cold snap. She added thin, black leather gloves and a cashmere scarf.

She indeed looked ready for a polar expedition—DC style. It would be hard to find a person more the opposite of Anne Darlington. Anne had looked storm-tossed when she'd retreated from Daniel's office wrapped deep in her massive parka. She'd frankly looked…miserable.

"Hit me with the short version."

"Seven a.m. breakfast with the present governor of Colorado. You asked me to specifically remind you not to call him an idiot."

But the man was.

"Simply because he doesn't agree with your prior policies," she read his expression easily of course, "does not necessarily reflect on his mental capacity."

"And yet he is."

She sighed and then nodded, her shoulder-length hair slid forward and back in a sharp slicing motion that emphasized her narrow face and dark eyes, "And yet he is. But your life at next month's fundraiser in Denver will be easier if you don't remind him of that."

"Got it. I'm going to make a call."

"Should I wait?" She already had her tablet out to make any notes he side-spoke to her.

"No. Go home for a change. Have some eggnog," and he briefly wondered what Cornelia Day did in her time off. Did she even have a life outside the office? "We're done for today."

She squinted at him momentarily. He could feel her attempting to peer inside his head and read his thoughts. He barely had a clear idea of them himself, so he wished her luck.

"Tomorrow morning," the slightly worried look didn't clear. "At the Hay-Adams, seven a.m."

At his nod, she moved off.

He crossed to one of the guard's desks. "Could you call the Residence for me? Third floor."

#

Anne wished Daniel would show up and answer his own damned phone; it had rung until she thought it might be a new and effective form of torture. She'd been on the verge of snatching it off the cradle anyway, her hand mere inches away when it had finally stopped.

She held her breath.

It didn't restart.

Counted to ten.

Still nothing.

She retreated to a seat in the Music Room at the top of the White House Residence and stared eastward. In the distance, a peek-a-boo view of the Capitol Building's dome was etched in yellow light against the darkening sky. The bronze Statue of Freedom atop the dome stood with her butt facing Anne; a fact she knew from past curiosity. Though the distance made it impossible to actually see the butt from here, she could feel it. Why wasn't this a surprise?

Tennessee. She'd just escaped Tennessee, but it was still awfully tempting to call the family plane to come right back and pick her up. Why did she think DC was going to be any better? Because it rhymed with Tennessee? Maybe she should try Gay Paree next—at least the number of syllables would match properly. All she needed was a time machine to take her back to 1920s Paris.

If she—

There was a discreet knock on the open Music Room door.

She glanced over her shoulder and then spun to her feet in surprise, almost catapulting herself to the floor. "Mr. Vice President."

"Team leaders are supposed to call me Zack. I'm fairly sure that was in the ship's articles."

"Typical Air Force, didn't read before signing. Why are you here, sir?" Not that she was complaining; she was inordinately pleased to see him. He was handsome, but not in the way of the President or her brother. There was a quietness to his face and a calmness in his bearing that the other two men lacked. He had thick hair, not long, but thick and nearly black. His light brown eyes were kind on an open face that reflected every emotion.

"Well, I tried calling, but you didn't answer the phone. Never going to get your expedition team put together if you don't pick up the phone when they call." He was leaning against the doorjamb in a comfortable slouch that not only made him look entirely pleasant, but also made her feel a little more relaxed.

"Not my phone. Though if I'd known it was you come a-calling, Mr. Vice President…" She would have…what?

"Well, it seems that we're stuck with the formality, doesn't it? Therefore I must ask myself what would cause Leader Darlington to relax?" He moseyed into the room; he really was from Colorado. Since when did a man mosey? When did it ever look so good?

Her pulse picked up a notch with each step he took toward her which was a completely ridiculous thing to happen.

He stopped a step away and looked down at her. "It seems that you have a problem, Ms. Darlington."

"I do?" Only a few thousand of them, but they were difficult to recall with him standing so close. Zachary Thomas was often listed atop those most-eligible-bachelor lists, not that she ever noticed such things. He was one of those rare men who had built a political career without being married or being eviscerated in the press when he did date.

"Yes," Zachary nodded to himself with a firm surety that didn't quite tip over into arrogance though it certainly was thinking about doing just that. "And I have the cure. Get your coat."

"I find that order a little preemptory for my taste, Assistant Expedition Leader Thomas. If you're taking me somewhere cold, you can find another victim."

"Somewhere warm, but you'll want the coat to get there. Besides, there's no point wearing such nice boots and not using them. They really are great boots."

She looked down at her cowboy boots. Classic Lucchese, understated dark-brown leather with elegant hand tooling and stitching. She used them hard, so they were a little battered, but soft as slippers on her feet. She'd mainly worn them to the White House to tease Daniel who had once lectured her for not wearing a nice dress and high heels when she visited. She hadn't worn high heels since her senior prom—when you were five-six, all heels did was make tall people think of you as a pretender. Of course tall women only wore them so that they could brag; Anne had banned them from her closet years ago.

She inspected Zack again. Maybe she'd just pretend to enjoy herself. If she did it long enough, it might catch on. But the military man needed to be taken down at least one peg.

"And the *order* to march?"

"Old captainly habits that will probably never change." At least he was honest about that.

She hooked her arm through his—a little alarmed at her own presumption, but not willing to look foolish by letting go immediately—and led him out into the Center Hall that stretched the length of the third floor.

"I'll need to fetch my coat. So, Air Force Captain?" she asked to cover her sudden nerves. "Is that good?"

# # #

Zack looked down at her in surprise. He always forgot how little civilians knew about the military. It almost made him regret this visit. But he remembered that lonely look as she'd left her brother's office and couldn't bear the thought of her sitting up here alone. Especially as Peter and Daniel still had a long list to cover before their day would be over.

"It's better than lieutenant, less than major."

"And nowhere near general. Too bad. I was hoping for a general."

"You wouldn't like it. Their star insignias are sharp and prickly."

"Whereas captain's bars aren't nearly as problematic? Which only matters if someone gets up close and personal," she let out a great mock sigh. "I was so hoping for a general."

He almost kept walking straight down the hall when she turned for a bedroom halfway down the north side. If she knew that a captain wore bars, she certainly knew where his former rank fell in the hierarchy of military officers. Zack made a mental note never again to underestimate Anne Darlington. And he had the sneaking suspicion that he would, many more times before he finally learned that lesson.

On the bed, an explosion had happened with only a small corner of a large knapsack protruding. She didn't travel with a fleet of suitcases and cosmetic bags and who knew what all women traveled with. By what was showing from the confused pile, she might have been heading out for the back country just as likely as visiting DC. He had the distinct impression that with Anne Darlington a man simply got what he saw without any games.

And once out of her parka, there was a great deal to like about what he saw. He'd watched her for a long moment before he'd knocked at the open Music Room door where she'd sat so still and at peace. She was neither some sleek urbanite like Cornelia nor a solid girl. Her cobalt turtleneck clung tightly to a balance of strength and femininity that he rather liked and he'd never quite seen so wonderfully melded before. When she'd spun to her feet in the Music Room and faced him, he'd been hard pressed not to do more than glance at her fine figure. Again neither sleek nor voluptuous, merely designed to rivet a man's attention if he had a single ounce of taste.

She gathered her parka and, turning, caught him staring at places he shouldn't be.

Mind out of the gutter, Zack. Daniel's sister. Yet he'd been the one to flirt with her, *prickly general's stars* indeed.

They picked up Harvey at the elevator—ex-football running back turned head of the Vice Presidential Protection Detail.

Impressively, Anne didn't flinch away. She must have become used to the tight security with her brother's escort.

As he and Harvey had ridden up to the third floor earlier, he'd warned Harvey that they might be going to the concert at the US Botanic Garden. It was perhaps the shortest notice he'd ever given to his security detail and he felt bad about that. But Zack wanted to surprise Anne Darlington. Wanted to see if he could erase that sadness. It didn't fit her well, like a bad choice in clothes. He still wasn't sure of the impulse that made him think he was the Santa who could wave his hand and suddenly she'd be cheerful once more, but he was here nonetheless.

He sighed. Actually, he knew where some of the impulse came, but getting on the wrong side of the White House Chief of Staff would not be a good idea.

"Harvey, please tell Chief of Staff Darlington that his sister has stepped out for a few hours." Which wouldn't begin to cover it if Daniel decided something inappropriate was going on, which there wasn't. He was merely taking a beautiful lady to somewhere warm, and a public concert.

And he decided to stop thinking about that either way before he was turning in circles worse than a helicopter with a shot-up tail rotor.

When the elevator reached the main lobby they picked up two more guards. Their dark suits and coats looked like dark blots on the explosion of cheer that had struck the Residence earlier in the day. Paper snowflakes the size of toboggans dangled from the ceiling. Trees almost invisible beneath storms of multi-colored ball ornaments cropped up around every corner. Any vertical feature, whether a column or archway, positively dripped with cheer. It was a very different White House than the years of Katherine Matthews or when a lonely President had lived here by himself.

They picked up another two agents plus a pair of SUVs when they reached their own vehicle. His traveling doctor and the serviceman carrying the Vice President's nuclear football—a non-descript leather satchel that contained forty pounds of the most effective communication equipment ever designed—rode in the trailing vehicle. Day or night, he was never supposed to be more than a few hundred feet from the football. One of his only two official duties: break a tie vote in the Senate and blow up the world if the President was out of commission and the US was attacked.

They climbed into their own SUV and the vehicle's heavy doors were slammed and locked. They would pick up the last of the escort at the outer gate.

"How many agents follow you around?" Anne's whisper barely reached him despite her sitting next to him in the back seat and the exceptional sound insulation provided by so many layers of armor.

"I'm afraid that's a state secret, Ms. Darlington. Strictly need-to-know."

"And I don't need to know. Don't even think I'd want to."

Her voice had become so small that he began to worry. A Secret Service escort was a daunting envelope to enter and he'd had five years practice, six if he included the run-up to the first election. "Truth be told, I don't know either. Unlike some protectees, I don't try to tell the Secret Service how to do their job."

"You were right though," her voice abruptly returned to normal as they headed out of the White House grounds and picked up a four-motorcycle escort.

"I was?"

"Shockingly, yes," and that initial teasing tone that had so captivated him at their first meeting finally returned.

"I'll alert the media. It's a first. Better yet, tell the President for me, would you? He'll be thrilled. What was I right about?"

"Getting out and about."

"I'm glad." *Yes,* he told himself, *being kind to a beautiful woman did work out sometimes.*

"So, these men and women all follow you wherever you choose to go?"

"They do."

"Excellent!" Anne slapped her gloved hands together. "We have a team now. North Pole here we come."

"That's a little farther than I planned for this evening."

"Spoilsport!" She may have stuck her tongue out at him, it was hard to tell with the little bit of streetlight that filtered through the tinted windows. "Could you at least have them turn up the heat so that it doesn't *feel* as if we're going there?"

That he could do.

# # #

Anne had assumed they were headed to some stuffy Washington museum or gallery that she'd already visited too many times on prior visits. She'd promised herself to present a happy face because it was a huge relief just to be out, under any circumstances, and away from her own whirling thoughts.

And it was deeply kind of Zachary Thomas. Rather daunted by the man escorting her, she'd gone right through panic and decided that her only chance at sanity now lay in the land of the ridiculous. The Darlington Polar Expedition had suddenly become the most rational part of her evening. A stuffy museum would get her back to reality soon enough.

But the first of the Smithsonian museums, then a second and a third were passed by. The National Gallery disappeared astern as well while their craft continued racing up the National Mall toward the Capitol Building. She'd thought a vehicle transporting the Vice President would be more…luxurious. Other than the surprisingly heavy doors—that she'd tried to close herself and was ultimately glad for the Secret Service agent's aid—the interior was no fancier than the Suburban they used on the farm to fetch important guests from the airport. However, the company now was stratospheric in comparison and her head was still spinning.

"Why are we going there?" She pointed up and ahead. "Lady Freedom has her butt facing me and I find that rather rude of her."

The Vice President ducked down and to the side to peer upward at the top of the Capitol dome. "How did I never notice that?"

"I thought men always paid attention to women's butts."

"Not when they're twenty stories up and made of bronze. Now, when they're as nice as y—" He bit off the words, but it was too late.

Harvey, the Secret Service agent in the front passenger seat, had a sudden coughing fit that sounded suspiciously like a laugh.

She didn't bother holding back and let her laugh loose. At least for a moment. It was cute that the Vice President had just been caught ogling her behind. It was even cuter that he was embarrassed. And then it struck her that he wasn't embarrassed because he'd been flirting; he had an obvious talent for that—one she appreciated and enjoyed returning. No, he was embarrassed because he had actually meant what he'd been about to say.

Anne started to ask the next question, but became very self-conscious of the two agents sitting in the front of the vehicle. Keeping her thoughts to herself earned her a couple of worried looks from Zack Thoma—*No!*—from the Vice President. Which thankfully was all he had time for before the agents announced their arrival.

She read the sign: United States Botanic Garden Conservatory. Large dark letters on a typical DC sandstone block building.

"Are you kidding me?" she turned back to the Vice President as the agent opened his door and he climbed out to the sidewalk. "It's night. The temperature is sub-Arctic. And you're taking me to tromp through a bunch of gardens coated in ice?" Even though she still sat on the far end of the back seat from his open door, the cold wrapped around her legs.

"The more fragile gardens are indoors," he had to lean down to continue speaking to her still in the car as she wasn't moving. "Trust me, they'll be warm enough for you to be removing your parka."

"So that you can ogle me some more?"

"I'll admit that is an advantage to the situation from my point of view. One that I assure you I hadn't thought of until this moment." His words sounded sincere, but she could see the hint of a smile exposed by the shining interior dome light that made her suspicious.

"Well at least you're owning up to it," and she didn't particularly mind that he wanted to; which was the interesting aspect of it for her. Usually men who stared irritated the crap out of her.

"Now can we move along?" He extended a hand, palm up, back into the car. "The Secret Service gets very nervous when I stand still out of doors, especially as this is an unscheduled visit."

If the Secret Service became nervous about having the Vice President exposed, then they were concerned about his safety... as in someone shooting him. She grabbed his hand and scooted out of the car. She was all set to drag him to the Conservatory's open doors. But she couldn't.

When she reached the sidewalk, she could finally see what the Suburban's roof had hidden. To her right loomed the massive dome of the Capitol Building with Lady Freedom's gowned backside on clear display. Directly in front of her, the Conservatory's massive front wall ended after a single story. Above it soared a myriad array of glass and steel greenhouses. There were angled ones, round ones, and in the front and center a gigantic tower of glass that rose a half dozen stories. Inside the glass were masses of foliage lit brightly from within like a science-fiction-in-space forest, all tucked safely beneath mighty glass domes that looked very Old World.

"If milady is quite done being a gaper..." Zack trailed off but the nudge was sufficient to get her moving. A circle of agents formed up close behind them and they hustled in.

"How do you learn to live with..." she waved a hand toward the dark night now safely on the other side of the closed doors, "...that?" Daniel's guard had always been fewer and looser on the rare occasions when they'd gone out on the town together. The size and tightness of the Vice Presidential Protection Detail emphasized the imminent threat that always surrounded him.

"You don't. At least I haven't. But we never talk about it either: the President, Daniel, or I. Odd, but there it is. Now, before us we have an adventure that requires neither sled dogs nor polar-worthy parkas," he waved toward a cloak room. "Shall we proceed?"

Anne sniffed the air tentatively. It was warm and didn't bite at the inside of her nose. It was also moist and rich with intriguing scents. The air hung thick with fresh soil, the clean scent of chlorophyll hard at work making oxygen, and foreign scents of strange plants.

While the building's facade had been nearly fortress-like, the interior was impossibly lush from the very first step. There were potted begonias dangling from the ceiling, thick with blooms despite the season. Massive variegated Algerian ivies of green-and-white reached up wrought iron lattices mounted on the walls, granite pathways led between planters thick with exotics where every step was a new adventure.

Anne had always thought she had a grip on at least the flora of the world around her. The Conservatory had been custom-designed to shatter that illusion. She knew food crops but these plants served no real purpose beyond being joyously cheerful. She would have felt sorry for them trapped in their Conservatory cage but that would lead to a dark place on her own account, so she focused on the plants instead.

Yellow iris and yellow azaleas she could pin down. The scarlet rosemallow and the African tulip tree she only needed a quick peek at the name placards. The flowers made of bright orange vertical petals with sprays of white cups springing out of them like tiny water fountains mystified her. Lollipop flower—*Pachystachys lutea*. Nope. Not even a clue. But it was a jungle flower and she'd never been to the jungle—at least not until now.

The jungle grew inside the primary greenhouse dome and massive trees climbed upward to fill the space. Nor were there simply unfamiliar trees. Their branches also supported other growing and flowering plants, dripping orchids, perky epiphytes, and hundreds of butterflies—they were like Christmas painted by an inspired elf with a palette of a thousand colors.

As promised, the heat and moisture were lush here and she felt warm for the first time since arriving in DC. There was a pleasant crowded closeness that was lacking in the American wilderness. The only close comparison she had was on a research trip she'd done into the Louisiana swamp and that had a dense, brooding feeling. Combined with a brutal heat and humidity, the swamp was her least favorite place ever.

The other thing that had happened without her noticing was that her hand had remained looped through the Vice President's arm the entire time. A time that had passed in a surprisingly comfortable silence.

She looked up at him, "You're a very pleasant man to be around, Mr. Vice President."

"And you've become a very quiet woman."

"Sorry, but I do like plants. Each has managed to find a niche and adapt to it. Every one has its own story and I find that fascinating. That the gardeners have managed to make them all coexist under glass in Washington DC is one of the closest things to a miracle it has ever been my good fortune to see."

"I thought you were trying to get away from the farm," his voice was a tease.

"That's different," and she could feel her shoulders tightening up in self-defense as if she was about to be battered by a foul winter storm. "Can we have a subject change?"

"How do you feel about model trains?"

"About what?"

He pointed down as a small train wove beneath the leaves of a massive poinsettia before trundling across a wooden bridge and ducking into a tree trunk.

"What's a train doing here?"

"Did you also miss the buildings?"

Anne followed his finger as he pointed. DC was on display here, but hidden. Intricate copies of dozens of landmarks worked in wood were tucked here and there among the foliage, tiny windows brightly lit from within. A reproduction of the Capitol Building stood not five feet away and she hadn't even noticed it among the incredible foliage.

"It's no more than knee-high to a rose bush."

The building's great mass had been reduced down, but it was intricate and elegant in dark wood rather than its true white stone. She leaned in and squinted at the tiny Statue of Freedom. "At least this time her butt isn't facing us." A different train trundled by—the engine blue rather than red this time and a long line of boxcars—looping around the Capitol before heading back the way it had come.

Then she glanced over at the Vice President. He was watching her. Not her body, but her face. And he was doing so with a look of surprise.

"What?"

"You really didn't notice all this? It's the best part of their yearly display. I try to never miss it."

"Played with trains a lot when you were a child?"

He faked an innocent look that didn't work at all. "Might have," then his face sobered. "The big layout in the basement was the only thing that Dad and I really did together growing up. Mostly me. He was deployed or here in DC most of the time."

"Why didn't you move here?"

"Mom's life is in the Springs. Her parents and friends are there. She's deeply involved with the Olympic Training Center as well—silver medal in freestyle swimming and a gold in team relay. It was hard on her when I followed in Dad's footsteps instead of hers, but I can only see that in retrospect. She encouraged me every step of the way. She was a good mom in a distracted sort of way; her life was at the OTC, not at home."

Anne hugged his arm briefly to her side in comfort. It felt so natural to be walking with him this way. Like the trains and model buildings, the Secret Service agents had blended into the background for her though they were only a few steps away. It helped that the agents were looking everywhere except at them. Once noticed, they were thoroughly daunting in the dark suits with their radio earpieces. That kept the other people milling down the walkways at bay as well. So it felt as if their conversation was truly private. She looked again.

"Why are there so few people here?"

"You mean other than it's a cold winter's night?"

"Yes, other than that."

"The Conservatory stays open this late only twice a week and only for the holiday concerts. Tonight it's The Congressional Hearings."

"Are they as boring as that sounds?"

Before the Vice President could answer a clear voice sounded in the distance. It was a single, high soprano note, that sounded sad and alone as it echoed down through the various habitats of the Conservatory. The opening phrase of *Silent Night* was incongruously wrong as it reached the warm jungle greenhouse.

Almost without thinking, she followed the sound with Zachary close beside her. Zachary. Some part of her had let go of "Mr. Vice President" and she'd have to be careful that it didn't escape out into the world. That would be too disrespectful. But internally she decided that she liked Zachary Thomas very much.

Silent Night led them down corridors thick with red, green, and white poinsettias, then through a passageway beneath an arch of massively blooming purple bougainvillea. The soprano was joined by a larger group of voices as *Good King Wenceslas* accompanied them past a miniature Jefferson Memorial, the Washington Monument, and a gorgeous model of the Conservatory complete with tiny plants and bonsai trees visible through the miniature greenhouse roofs. And now that she was looking for them in their tour, the constant hum of trains was everywhere as they clattered around tree trunks and ducked out of sight under banana leaves bigger than the length of whole trains.

Zachary Thomas playing with trains in the basement. It was easy to imagine him so, despite his lofty office. Even easier to imagine him with a child or two to join him.

They reached the main Garden Court where they'd first entered, looking almost sparse now after touring through the jungle's lush growth. A small stage had been backed against the main entrance. The aisles had sprouted folding chairs in every nook and cranny. There were perhaps a hundred of them, mostly filled.

On the small stage a dozen men and women crowded close together. Three of the women wore sparkling red gowns, the other three an elegant green. The men, typically, had it easy and all wore very sharp-looking black tuxedos. At first she thought they were a choir, but spotted no violin or percussion though she could hear them clearly. Acapella. One of the men was beat-boxing a drum kit with his voice and a woman trilled like a fine set of strings to accompany the other voices. The effect was magical.

Zachary guided her to a pair of seats at the very back, close by an exit. The Secret Service agents arranged themselves in doorways and stood against the back wall, only Harvey remaining close by—clearly ready to throw himself in front of the Vice President in case there was mad caroler in the crowd.

She could see the effects of the Vice President's presence propagate slowly forward through the crowd. One head turned, then another. In moments the back half of the audience was glancing their direction, barely watching the concert.

"Zachar—Mr. Vice President?" she asked him softly. All of the attention was unnerving her.

"It's okay, Anne."

She'd almost used his name. A heat rose to her cheeks that was partly from the crowd's attention but partly from her own presumption.

"They'll get used to it in a moment."

She didn't like being looked at so much. But after a few whispered comments between companions, most turned away. Some waved. The Vice President waved back pleasantly, but quickly returned his attention to the concert. More than one of them snapped a photograph.

A photo of the Vice President.

No, of the Vice President and…

"We have to go," she whispered fiercely and started to rise.

"Why?" he kept her in place by wrapping his other hand over where hers was still tucked inside his elbow.

"They're taking pictures."

"They always do," the Vice President remained perfectly calm, keeping his voice soft enough to not disturb anyone on the other side of the two-seat buffer that the Secret Service was maintaining to all sides.

"They're taking pictures of *us*. Don't you get that?"

"My dear Ms. Darlington, they've been doing that since the moment we stepped into the Conservatory."

"They have? But the media…" How had she not noticed that? Was she so oblivious?

"You mean the *social* media—ten times faster I assure you, though curiously it is generally kinder. I am single. I have been known to escort beautiful women before, though none quite as startling as you. It will give them something to talk about."

"The only thing startling about me is how out of my depth I am."

On the farm she'd have noticed someone pulling out a camera. Visitors to the farm always wanted a photo with one of the Darlingtons, but it was done with a Southern politeness and they almost always asked first. Here there must have been a thousand surreptitious snaps with camera phones. It would be all over DC already. Picked up by the national media by tomorrow and…

"I'm so not ready for this."

# # #

Zack felt contrite, but not very. This sort of attention was mild compared to when he took someone to a restaurant or other public venue. He considered leaving as Anne had suggested, but he didn't want to. He was enjoying the music; the group was very good, though their current early Baroque Christmas ballad was less to his taste. And he was very much enjoying her company. She had used his name rather than his title with an easy familiarity that few women achieved and never on a first date; well, almost had.

Date?

Yes. It felt like a first date. And a good one if he was any judge. Her hand still remained lightly trapped between his own and his elbow. He liked that as well.

She wasn't one of the typical DC women he was used to—who were very focused, very goal-oriented. Over the last five years he'd briefly dated a State Department senior analyst, a Judicial Branch mediator, and a serving Air Force captain from the Pentagon's Southeast Asia division. Everyone was driven by a force that the Coloradan in him found exhausting. There was never a down moment. There was never only one thing on the table. And all of that was backed by the directness of a DC insider that left room for little else.

When Anne had concentrated on the plants, she'd looked at nothing else. She had no agenda, hidden or otherwise. Her questions when they spoke weren't about politics. In his world, he had to watch every word he said because it could be used by his date later to make a cutting point or to feed the media. Instead of speaking with infinite caution, he'd told Anne Darlington about the train set.

He'd never told anyone about that, not even childhood friends who would have gone nuts if they'd seen the elaborate setup in the Thomas' basement. It had been his and his father's alone. Zack had spent endless hours building miniature landscapes, shaping two-percent grades, and forming tunnels through tiny mountains. They'd used the smallest train gauge—the tiny Z, where a seventy-foot engine was reduced to a mere four inches long—allowing for the maximum complexity in the space they had—a twenty-story building scaled to just under a foot high in the Z-gauge world. Whenever General Thomas had come home, Zack had barely been able to contain himself until after that first night's dinner when just the two of them would go down and inspect the results of Zack's efforts.

His father might spend half an hour inspecting all the changes if he'd been away for a long time. He'd run trains over any new sections and they'd both check for performance and realism. The general's highest form of praise would be when he rolled up his sleeves and say, "Looks as if we're ready to start the next section."

Zack came to the Conservatory each year not for the concerts, or even the models of DC landmarks, but instead for the trains. They were mostly the bigger O-gauge, whose eighteen-inch long engines always felt clunky to him, but still they were very well done. It made him both nostalgic and a bit sad; which were the two emotions he most associated with Christmas.

His father was presently stationed at the Eglin Air Force Base in Florida but was often in DC. Their few dinners together were awkward, quiet, and now very infrequent. That his own son might someday be the next Commander-in-Chief had raised another wall of formality, as if there hadn't already been enough since the day Zachary Thomas had entered the academy and become a very junior officer who saluted every time his father appeared.

Yet he'd told Anne Darlington about the trains. She was smart, beautiful, and funny—the last something he definitely wasn't used to. She also offered a genuine warmth that made her stand out even more from his prior experiences.

The Congressional Hearings' rendition of *I Saw Mama Kissing Santa Claus* had him looking over at Anne. She was singing along silently, again simply in the moment. He almost leaned down to...but they were in public and he had no wish to embarrass her further. Never before had he needed to think about keeping any physicality carefully out of sight behind closed doors. Anne made him think again.

All he'd expected was a pleasant evening spent cheering her up. Instead, he was on a first date and wondering like an overeager teen if he might get a kiss at the end of the evening. The group broke into a racy rendition of *All I Want for Christmas Is You*.

She happened to glance up at him and immediately started laughing. Her merry tone loud enough to make several of the nearer concert goers turn to look.

"What?"

Anne patted his arm in a friendly fashion, "It's all over your face, Mr. Vice President."

He considered doing his best to fix that. Then he thought better of it and rubbed his hand all over his face as if trying to erase any expression. When he finished, he made a goofy face with a sloppy grin.

"Is this any better?"

"Much!" And her continued merriment verified that as true.

He did school his expression after he heard the *ka-shick* sound of several cell phones.

Chapter 3

Of course they chose that picture."

Anne was not going to give her brother the satisfaction of appearing put out by the newspaper he was waving around. His wife Alice was paying very careful attention to her bowl of fruit and yogurt.

They were sitting on stools in the Residence's third floor kitchen around the large maple cutting block island. She'd always liked this kitchen, it was elegant but cozy—dark-stained oak cabinets with brass hardware. If she ever had a house of her own, it would have a kitchen like this one. Alice wore jeans, a turtleneck, and a knit sweater in Christmas red with a complex white snowflake worked into the back. Daniel wore his inevitable three-piece suit. This President was more informal than most, often found in no more than a shirt and tie with his suit pants, but not his Chief of Staff.

"I think it's cute," Anne just couldn't leave it alone: Zachary's face distorted like a circus clown's, her own head back in the moment of the laugh she'd been unable to repress.

"*VP Fools Around With*…double-entendre intended… *Unidentified Blond*," Daniel read the headline aloud for the fifth time, each time with the same notation. Her brother always was a little predictable.

Alice didn't speak but pointed her spoon toward the small television on the counter tuned to CNN, but with the sound off. Anne's own picture, not a bad one thank god, was on the screen. Large white letters on a red background read, *White House Chief of Staff's Sister.*

"No longer unidentified. Don't I even get my own name?"

"Not in this city," Alice smiled at her. "Even if I hadn't taken Daniel's last name, it wouldn't have mattered. At the CIA I'm typically referred to as the W-H-C-o-S wife. That's pronounced whickos, like whackos. You learn to roll with it."

"Why did you take my brother's name anyway? I always meant to ask."

"I just love him that much," she smiled sweetly at Daniel.

Anne made a gagging sound.

"I also wanted to anchor firmly in his subconscious that this is permanent. I only give my heart once."

"Don't have to worry about that. My brother is more loyal than a herd of lemmings."

"He is. So are you, which is a very sweet family trait. So, when are you going to tell your brother what kind of a kisser the Vice President is?"

"Why would I tell him about tha—" And Anne knew that she'd walked right into Alice's trap. She had to remember that Alice Darlington III was a top analyst and nothing slipped by her despite the impression given by her casual attire and cheerfully unruly mop of russet-colored hair that often hid one or other eye from view.

"You…kissed…the…Vice…President?" Daniel finally slumped onto his stool, his power-smoothie still untouched before him.

"He kissed me."

"Details, Sister," Alice ignored her husband's sputtering. "I want details."

"Okay, maybe I kissed him. But he's such a gentleman that sometimes the girl has to take the initiative."

"Don't I know it," Alice sighed and spooned up some more yogurt. "Your brother has the same issue."

"I kissed you first."

"Yes!" Alice suddenly cried out. "I was exhausted. Out on my feet. He took wholly inappropriate advantage of me. Threw me onto this very counter and ravaged me senseless."

"I did no such thing!"

"Regrettably true," Alice's voice returned to absolute normal. "And no matter how he remembers it, I had to kiss him first; though he did get with the program very quickly. Still—me, this counter, wild sex—never happened."

Anne only had to look in Alice's eyes for a moment before they both turned to Daniel and said in unison, "Why not?"

They both turned away and left Daniel to sputter pointlessly on a new topic.

To save Alice repeating her question about the kiss, because there was no question she would, Anne continued, "What skills the Vice President might lack in maintaining proper decorum in public," she tapped the newspaper Daniel had dropped onto the cutting block, "he more than compensates for in the back seat of a Secret Service SUV parked safely out of sight in the EEOB garage."

"My own sister kissed the Vice President…" Daniel's voice was soft and disbelieving.

"Drink your smoothie, dear," Alice patted his hand.

Momentarily quelled, he did just that. Alice really was impressive in how she could handle her brother. He'd always been the polite sibling, but he'd also been stubborn to the edge of monomania whenever he was locked onto a topic.

Anne still didn't quite believe that kiss herself.

Only one of the agents had actually left the vehicle, stepping out to open her door, when she'd done it. Harvey had remained in the SUV.

Still seated, she and Zachary had both stumbled over "pleasant evening" words and then relapsed into silence. It wasn't that he'd been so kind to her that made her decide to kiss him; it was that he simply was so kind. What she wasn't going to tell her sister-in-law, or her brother for that matter, was that the goodnight kiss had been intended as only a friendly peck of thanks on the cheek. Let them think it had been little more than that.

But it hadn't happened that way. As if by some unspoken plan, he'd turned just as she leaned in and in seconds she was lost in a kiss that had her practically crawling into his lap for more. Perhaps she would have if either of them had thought to release their seat belts. Zachary Thomas' kisses didn't allow much room for thought; all she'd been able to do was feel. And the feeling had been glorious right down to her toes. Before they came up for air, Harvey also had exited the vehicle—without her even noticing.

Oh, there was something else she'd almost forgotten.

Anne winked at Alice, then she turned to face Daniel, "By the way, Brother, I have dinner plans tonight."

# # #

The rap on his front door was in the rhythm that Zack recognized as Harvey's.

He continued dictating instructions to Cornelia over his shoulder as he came out into the front foyer. Normally he would just shout that it was open—the ever present Secret Service a better guard than any deadbolt—but he had hopes on who he'd find there. He saw two images through the frosted glass: the tall, square-shouldered head of his Protection Detail and a shorter, lighter image that just had to be Anne. He opened the heavy door himself.

"Wow! What a beautiful house. I love the three-story circular turret." But she wasn't looking at the interior, she was looking at him, which had his body reheating rapidly with the memory of her kiss last night. Just like Anne herself, there had been nothing tentative about it. No considerations of composure or propriety. She'd apparently wanted to kiss him as much as he wanted to kiss her, so she had. It had been amazing.

"Thanks," was all he managed. Her long spill of blond hair was back in a ponytail. Not one of those high-tails that were so in fashion and looked more like a hair extension than it did like hair, but a normal tail that just gathered her hair back from her face. And though she was once again in her voluminous parka, he now knew something of what lay hidden beneath those folds. Still showing jeans and those scuffed high-end cowboy boots below; definitely his kind of girl. She looked—

"Planning to invite me in or do Harvey and I have to stay out here in the cold until you are through with your military inspection, Captain Vice President sir?" She offered a sloppy salute.

"If I let you in, I may not let you leave again."

"Forewarned is disarmed. If you let me in, I may not *want* to leave again," her smile was sassy though she spoke completely matter-of-factly. "Besides, it's cold out here."

"I'll risk it," he held the door wide. Anne walked in. Harvey began to turn away. "Come in, Harvey, get warm for a minute. Cornelia's almost through for the day. Then if you could escort her back out through the gate, I'd appreciate it."

"Yes, sir, thank you. As Ms. Darlington may have remarked in much more colorful terms on the way here, it's cold enough to freeze a sled dog's behind tonight."

Zack shared a look with him.

Harvey stepped part way in then stopped. The head of his Protection Detail looked over Zack's shoulder and whispered quietly, "Incoming, sir." Taking a step backward, he closed the front door with himself on the outside and Zack inside.

He turned to see what had made a top Secret Service agent go into full retreat.

Anne stood in the center of the foyer with one arm out of her parka, not waiting for him to assist her. But she was frozen in place facing the Living Room archway in the awkward position of shoulder and elbow still raised even though the coat had slid free on that side.

Just stepping into the far side of the hall, Cornelia came out to see who the new arrival might be. There couldn't be a greater contrast in two women.

Anne as five-six of healthy and vigorous Tennessean. From the back he could see Anne's ponytail was held by a black rubber band. And she'd opted for no more than a well-tailored black denim shirt that matched her designer jeans. She looked modern and ready to join one of Mom's Olympic swimming teams.

"Hello, I've *read* so much about you," Cornelia, of course, smoothing the way with her perfect manners.

# # #

Anne thought about trying out a crushing-guy-grip thing, but it would fracture the woman's perfect manicure. Cornelia's cool gaze assessed and discarded Anne as a hick from the wilderness. This was exactly the sort of woman she'd expect the Vice President to be with—long, cool, and elegant. And he was with her, clearly Anne's arrival had interrupted something. So what was she doing here if he already had—

"She's my assistant. My right hand," the Vice President stepped forward. "Anne this is Cornelia Day. This is Dr. Darlington's sister, Anne Darlington."

"A pleasure," Cornelia spoke with all the warmth of the December evening, dark and bitter on the other side of the door. Assistant or not, she was dancing along the thin edge of rude. Anne had obviously trampled on forbidden territory.

Cornelia was six-one of DC elegant—not a hair out of place and her silk blouse perfectly complemented both her complexion and the Merino wool slacks that reached down to her two-inch heels: so five-foot-eleven of Cornelia and two inches of Kate Spades. She looked ready to take on a shark—either the aquatic or the legal kind—and there would be no doubting the victor in any contest. In the elegant reception hall of the Vice Presidential residence, Cornelia looked the perfect hostess. And before her, Anne felt as if she'd been beamed down from another world onto the center of the immaculate white Persian carpet to be glared at by Kennedy and the two Roosevelts.

One Observatory Circle was an elegant 1800s mansion built on the grounds of the National Observatory. She'd been captivated by the wide verandah that wrapped around the house. She'd gathered a few facts about it from the Secret Service agent who Daniel had insisted on sending rather than letting her take a cab. She'd been in dozens of the finest homes across the South. Many had far more pretention than this home, but few had such perfection and such artifacts.

"It's Dr. Melanie Anne Darlington, actually," a fact Anne typically played down. And in these elegant surroundings, she sounded pretentious but she couldn't stop herself.

Cornelia faced her directly, her shoulders squared beneath her Armani jacket. "Dr. Darlington. Bachelors in English Literature. MBA. Doctorate in Plant Sciences. All at University of Tennessee." She'd obviously done her homework.

"Yes," Anne acknowledged. "Valedictorian in all cases, you might add."

"I'm just a USAF captain—retired," Zachary chimed as if oblivious to the battle forming up in his front foyer. "That leaves me out of the running in this high-powered room."

Anne reached for a sense of humor in the situation, but had trouble finding it at first. Then she did, "Well, one of the three of us is also Vice President of the United States. I'm not sure that actually counts for much, but it must be worth something. Perhaps you can barter it for a free ice cream at the Lincoln Memorial."

Zachary nodded, "I hadn't thought of trying that. I'll give it a go next time I'm there."

But Cornelia Tight-ass scowled at Anne's light tone. Apparently even making fun of the Vice Presidential office was forbidden.

Then the Vice President changed topics as if nothing was going on. "Cornelia, in the briefing package for the climate meeting, I need a breakdown of each of the G-20's actual conservation efforts in the last decade. Hard numbers, not guesses from some analyst who doesn't give a damn."

She produced a tablet computer in an expensive red leather case that was as elegant as she was and made a notation.

"I think that's it."

"Very good, sir," she walked to the coat closet as if she was completely at home here. But Anne was secretly pleased that she did so with all the stiffness of the stick they had each just rammed up the other's butt.

Anne was glad for the thick white area rug that covered much of the hall because the way Cornelia was walking, her heels would have worked like jackhammers on the hardwood flooring that showed around the edges. Each step shook her slender frame with its intensity.

At the door she turned for what Anne feared was one last scathing attack, but all she said was, "Eight a.m. meeting with the Speaker on the Hill, Mr. Vice President. Good night, sir."

When the door closed, Anne sighed with relief. "Is she really gone?"

The Vice President didn't answer, but remained staring at the inside of the door.

Anne moved up beside him so that they could stare at it together.

"I certainly didn't see that coming," he said softly.

"I thought you didn't see it at all."

"Not blind, Dr. Darlington," then he grimaced at the door. "Well, not completely blind. Cornelia has been with me for seven years and never gave me a single signal."

Anne was on the verge of calling him blind again, but decided in favor of a far softer, "Well, you've been given a clear signal now, I'd say." She'd have gone for it with her brother, but it wasn't nice to kick a Vice President when he was down.

He nodded his agreement reluctantly.

"Are you sure you want me to stay? At some point I'm going to be gone again," or fall off the edge of the planet, "and you clearly depend on her."

He shook it off and turned from the door to face her but she could still see the concern remaining.

"No, please stay. Besides, I'm guessing…" then he smiled, abruptly at ease. "I'd lay three-to-one odds that I'm not the one in the doghouse here."

"That makes no sense at all."

He took her parka and carried it to the front closet. "I rather think it's about *you* not being good enough for *me*. I've dated before and never had this reaction from her."

Anne certainly hoped that's what it was. She wasn't even good enough for herself and she'd come to terms with that…or was trying to. At least that was a playing field she understood.

"You know what I need, Mr. Vice President?"

"What, Dr. Darlington?"

"I need a beer. Please tell me that you don't just have white wine."

"Yes!" He pumped a fist in the air. "If you tell me that you like football, I'm *not* letting you leave."

"College or pro?" It was an important question among football fans.

"College of course," his smile was electric for her knowing there was a distinction in the first place. "The Air Force Academy Falcons."

"Might have watched a game or two…in which the Tennessee Volunteers totally tromped their flyboy behinds," Anne crowed with delight and began feeling much better about how the evening was going. "Seem to recall a total choke back in 2006." The two teams were in different conferences, so the meet-ups were few and far between.

"One point. Give me break. We went for the two-point conversion—"

"And missed it! And don't even get me going on the 1971 Sugar Bowl, 34 to 13."

Zachary groaned as if it was yesterday even though neither of them had been alive back then. "We tromped the Army this year," he offered as a lame recovery. "Just like I bet we did to Stanford last night. I recorded the game but haven't watched it yet. Do *not* tell me."

"I would nev-ah," she placed an offended hand upon her chest in mock horror. "But it may or may not have been just like what the Navy did when they whupped your behinds last month," she slapped the verbal football back down in his turf.

He stopped and looked down at her, "How did you know all that?"

She offered her best smile, "It's either because I'm a Southern football genius or it's because I can use the Internet just as well as Ms. Cornelia Day." Or because she had a younger cousin on the Navy team. "The key question you should be focusing on at the moment, Mr. Vice President, is the location of my beer."

# # #

Once they'd crossed through the formal Dining Room into the Pantry Kitchen for a couple of tall cold ones, Zack led her on a tour of the house. As soon as the words, "It's in the Queen Anne style," were out of his mouth, he stopped using any other name for her. As with everything else, she simply took being dubbed "Queen Anne" in stride.

"I always did want to be queen for a day."

True to the form popular in the late 1800s, the first floor had few hallways and fewer doors, one room simply opened onto the next. The broad veranda curved around the cylindrical three-story turret that defined the southeast corner of the house. On the first floor, the circular room extended off the Living Room.

"The Christmas tree is usually in that nook of the Reception Hall; they move out the grand piano," he pointed with the neck of his bottle. "This year I had them put it here in the turret. I like the way the lights reflect off all of the windows."

"And I see that's the sole decorating decision you've made about the house in the five years you've been here."

"Perhaps." He looked around. The mansion was exactly as he'd received it. White area rugs with understated floral designs, stark white couches and chairs, and muted wallpaper that—now that he thought about it—made it feel more like a museum than a home. Without anyone to share it with, he hadn't been motivated him to make it a home. It wasn't something his family had much skill at.

He led her back through the Reception Hall, past the elegant staircase that climbed up through the core of the house in successive turns, and into the Library—the only room he really used other than the bedroom. His sole mark here was the half dozen shelves of thriller novels he read when he was too sick of State Department reports. He thought about the upstairs, he hadn't even changed the quilt that had been on the master bed. "Okay, more than perhaps."

"Same problem I have. Couldn't care in the least."

Again Zack was left to scratch his head in Queen Anne's wake. Each of the women he'd dated had said almost identical things on entering the house, "It's so beautiful. There's so much you could do with it." Even the ever-practical Cornelia had made a few comments about the availability of other furnishings from whatever department took care of such things. He had exchanged the JFK portrait between the bookshelves with a picture from home, but that was all he'd done.

Anne simply didn't care.

The Library was the most comfortable room in the house. There was room for a sofa and several armchairs. Arches led to the Reception Hall and Living Room with a small doorway leading into the Garden Room. He'd never been much of a one for plants, but some Navy steward had maintained it well enough for Anne to remark, "Nice."

To the north was a broad bay window looking out over the Observatory grounds during the day. To the south stood the bookcases and a television. If he wasn't entertaining, this was where he spent most of his time at home.

On one shelf he had a half dozen pictures that Anne had stopped in front of. He moved up behind her, close behind her, and enjoyed the feeling that they were almost embracing— definitely close enough to...

Seeking distraction, he looked over her head, "The family."

"I can see them both in you. Are they close?"

"As close as they want to be, I suppose. Which means if either one fell off the edge of the world, the other might or might not notice. They're both quite driven people in their own, deeply separate fields."

"And you became Vice President by sitting around on your lazy behind."

"Absolutely! Best method there is. Also, I should warn you that I was always the black sheep of the family, caring about people as people rather than for their roles on the ever-precious team." She didn't glance up at the surprising amount of bitterness that had slipped into his tone, having instead the courtesy to let him recover his equilibrium without comment.

In an unconsciously smooth sideways move she shifted from the narrow space between himself and his family photographs, to inspect the one larger picture from home—the one that had usurped JFK's place of honor. He had to smile at himself, don't underestimate Queen Anne Darlington.

She had just given him the space to recover; as wholly conscious a movement as him sidling close behind her in the first place.

"Is this a real train yard or your model?"

Even his father had not picked up on that. Zack had spent hours making sure every detail of his miniature train yard had been perfect, hazing the photo just enough to make it art rather than a model railroader's brag piece. He was inordinately proud of that image, but it also made him a little sad as he'd never had anyone to share it with.

When he didn't answer her, she looked at him, directly at him for the first time since when she'd crossed over the front threshold. She didn't speak, but just studied him.

"What?" His throat had suddenly gone dry.

"I think Mr. Vice President that it is dangerous for two such lonely people to stand here in such silence."

Lonely? But he was almost never alone. His typical day ran from seven a.m. to seven p.m. Late evenings he often as not had dinner meetings or reports to study, phone calls to return to earlier time zones to garner favor for a key piece of legislation, or...

"Lonely?" he managed a whisper but it didn't sound like much of a question.

"I think we have two choices," Anne remained serious and, unlike usual, he couldn't detect any hidden smile waiting with a joke.

"Which are?"

"You had mentioned a Falcons' game you recorded. Option one, we can sit on that couch and watch it." This is where he usually watched games and somehow Anne had figured that out. Sitting close beside her was an attractive option. He could see them laughing together over pizza, beer, and touchdowns—could see it very easily.

"Or?"

"Or," she took a very deep breath that caused some very nice shifts down her body that he did his decent best to ignore. "Or, we can just acknowledge where this is going and you can show me where the Vice President sleeps."

Zack Thomas had received many offers of sex over the years: some coy, some blatant, some little classier than a street walker's offer. He didn't think that he'd ever in his life received a more sincere offer than Anne's forthright statement.

He knew that with her it wasn't an offer of sex, it would be so much more than that. He didn't need to answer.

She stepped up to him and slipped the beer bottle from his fingers. She set both of them on coasters on the low white coffee table, then she held out her hand. When he took it, her touch was cool with condensation from the barely touched bottle, but her clasp remained firm as he led her to the central stairs and up into his bedroom.

# # #

Anne had not planned on ending up here. Hadn't even thought about it. But looking at the train picture, something had shifted deep inside for her. The care it must have taken. Every car had been meticulously real despite its tiny size. The rail yard hadn't merely been a clustering of narrowly-spaced parallel tracks. Instead tiny bits of gravel little bigger than sand grains had been spread all through the yard. Switching lights, yard workers, and even a tiny lone dog sniffing a wheel of the foremost engine. She could only imagine what it took to be the boy who'd done that.

When Zack reached for the light, she stopped his hand. Outside the winter might be cold, but it was also clear and the moon was a bright slash on the thick carpeting. In the room's warmth, the cold light warmed as well. Keeping their hands joined, she turned to face him and rested her other hand on his chest.

"This would be a good time to kiss me, Mr. Vice President."

"I'm not so sure about that," he nuzzled her hair. "Isn't it a bit presumptuous of me to think of bedding the expedition leader? Sounds like a court-martial offense to me. I want to approach this cautiously."

"If it's going to be your last night on earth, I'd suggest we enjoy it."

"You may have a point. Tonight we make love, for…" His hand was stroking her hair. With only one small snag, he freed it from the rubber band. He leaned down to kiss her where neck and her shirt's collar met beneath her freed hair.

"…tomorrow we might freeze to death. Or Cornelia might have me killed." She allowed her own hands to admire the softness of his beard, his strong jaw, and trace down over his very nice chest.

"Or Daniel might convince the President to send me on an extended tour of darkest Florida to be eaten by alligators." He mumbled into her ear.

"Don't miss Disney World as you head south. It's great fun," she loosened his tie, slipped it off his head, and at an opportune moment, slid it over hers.

"I was thinking more of Wolf Creek Pass." He removed her blouse and the bra followed quickly after. His lightest touch made her want more, his caresses were intense enough to unbalance her soul.

"What's that?" Anne had the sneaking suspicion that they weren't going to make it the last few steps to the bed.

"Ski area," he'd knelt and mumbled through his first kiss, which was between her breasts. "First to open in Colorado every year. Great place for Arctic training."

"Sounds cold," it would be if the room weren't so warm because the rest of her clothes had disappeared while she was appreciating this shoulder of the former soldier now kneeling before her.

"Lodge has hot cocoa and greasy French fries in front of a big fireplace."

"I've never skied, so I'll wait for you in the lodge. Greasy fries sound good," she knelt as well and tipped her head back to give him better access as his lips explored her shoulder. She wasn't in the mood for waiting for anything. She had thought they'd have a slow, loving experience. But the only reason she didn't drag him to the floor was that he was now headed there and dragging her down with him. She leaned down over him as he finally lay exposed in a patch of moonlight, seeking the kiss they'd never quite gotten around to.

He stopped her an inch away, holding her easily aloft with a hand on each shoulder.

She again tried to close the narrow gap that separated them, but still he resisted.

"You've never skied?"

"I've also never bedded a Vice President of the United States. So let me go if you want to be the first." She leaned in again, but still he kept them easily separated.

"You have to have skied."

"I've also never flown a fighter jet or swum across an ocean. Is that going to make you cast me from your bedroom?" He was working his way toward a sharp nudge in the ribs.

"We'll have to fix that you've never skied," the moonlit expression on his face remained serious. "It's important."

"Why? To see how fast I can turn into an icicle?"

"No," he brushed one hand down from her shoulder, over her breast and hip sending a shiver of need through her. "Because it is the only thing I can see standing between you and perfection."

With the same easy strength that he'd used to keep her at bay, he pulled her in, and she didn't fight him one tiny little bit. Perfection was about the farthest thing from Anne Darlington, but if this beautiful man wanted to believe otherwise, she'd do her best to convince him that he was right.

She also had been right the first time. Making love to Vice President Zachary Thomas for the first time was neither a hot nor fast event. It was slow, gentle, and made her feel as if maybe, just maybe, she had discovered a small corner of perfection herself.

Chapter 4

Why are you wearing a tie?"

"Oh," Anne brushed her hand down the smooth silvery silk of it. "Isn't it pretty?"

Daniel looked at her strangely, blinked twice, and then his face froze and she couldn't read his expression. That was unusual; she could always read what her brother was thinking. Or rather had been able to. He rose from his desk and closed the door to his office before returning. He sat beside her rather than circling back to his own side of the paper mountain.

"Don't start, little brother. I'm feeling too good for one of your lectures."

"That's Zack Thomas' tie."

"Vice President Zachary Thomas," she corrected and Daniel blanched at his slip into inappropriate familiarity. "He gave it to me and I find myself unwilling to return it yet."

"Melanie Anne…"

"Daniel Drake Darlington the Third…" she could match his threatening tone any day.

"I don't care if you're screwing Vice President Thomas—"

"You don't?" That stopped them both for a long moment, but he was the first one to recover.

"Okay, I do. But that's not the point. How many people have seen you while wearing that tie? I'm not the only one who would recognize it; that's one of his favorites."

She hadn't thought about that. She had worn it all through their long night together—wrestling in bed, eating ice cream and watching the football game while curled together on the Library couch at three in the morning. It had been the only clothing either of them had worn through the long night. And when they'd only made it back up to the second landing in the stairs where, with no protection close to hand, they'd had to improvise, she had found a few interesting uses for it. And this morning she'd slipped the neck loop under the fold of her denim collar and snugged it up properly. She'd never worn a man's tie before but it was far better than nylons on any day of the year.

"Maybe nobody else noticed?"

"Shall we find out, big sister?" Daniel almost sounded nasty. It wasn't really in him to succeed at such an endeavor, but he tried. He picked up a remote control and turned on one of the several televisions he had in his office.

And there was her picture. It was a long shot, through a major telephoto with all of its blurriness and foreshortening effects. But it was unmistakably her, in her big parka with the front still open because she was still near heat stroke from the thoroughness of Zachary's parting caresses. And, as the commentator was helpfully indicating with circles and arrows and a scrolling line below, there was the same tie that the Vice President had been wearing the prior day.

Next were side-by-side photos of Zack yesterday and of her coming in through White House security not twenty minutes ago. Again the same tie.

Well, the hog was in the waller now. No easy way to get it back out.

"Top item on the seven a.m. news," Daniel complained. "Ahead of Russia, ahead of the Japanese yen. Do you have any idea what trouble this is going to cause him? I don't even know where to begin to—"

She was trying to cut him off when the door to Daniel's office swung open and the President strode in already in mid-sentence, "Is that really Zack's tie on—"

He stopped. Frozen still when he spotted her.

Anne flapped the tie at him.

"Huh," the President grunted in a way that he'd never have done on national TV. "I guess it is."

He inspected her for a long moment, "How are you feeling, Anne?"

"You mean other than my little brother throwing a Southern-fried hissy fit?"

"Yes," he smiled down at her. "Other than that."

That's when she belatedly realized she was still sitting and scrambled to her feet along with Daniel. "My body is, well, Mr. President, rather pleased with the situation. My brain is as confused as—" she re-chose her words in mid-sentence, "—a chicken at a hog-calling contest."

Oddly enough that seemed to tickle him immensely as he smiled at some grand joke that only he was in on. "That's normal, then. Okay."

He considered a moment longer as he inspected her through narrowed eyes, then he clapped his hands together with some clear decision. "You all are having dinner in the Residence tonight. Daniel, would you let Zack and our wives know?" And he was gone.

Anne looked at the now empty doorway then back to her brother, "I thought I was confused before he walked in. What is he so all fired pleased about?"

"I don't know," Daniel settled slowly back into his seat. "But what it does mean, big sister, is that we're having dinner with the President and First Lady tonight. Please wear a dress."

"I didn't bring one." Had never needed one because she'd never had dinner with the President before, nor slept with the Vice President—two firsts in less than twenty-four hours. She was on a roll.

Daniel narrowed his eyes at her, then called out toward his still open office door, "Janet, I need someone to take my sister out clothes shopping. Then get a message to the Vice President and the First Lady about dinner."

Anne was going to offer to tell Zachary; it would also give her a chance to apologize for any trouble this was causing. Then she realized that she had no idea how to get in touch with the Vice President.

She headed for the door.

"Would you please take that damn tie off?"

She thought about it, then nodded toward the television. "I think that dog has already slipped the leash, don't you?"

# # #

Zack had been in meetings all day. The peremptory invitation to dine at the White House arrived in the same sixty-second break in which Cornelia filled him in on "Tie Gate." There were times he hated President Nixon and then there were times he just pitied the man. Every DC disaster for the last forty years had been tied back to his screw-ups at Watergate. Zack wondered if he himself should feel honored that his private life had been added to the legacy.

As his day progressed, he caught up with more photos of Anne Darlington as she traveled about DC. He had to give the woman points, she'd worn his tie proudly every step of the way. It looked damn good on her.

However, he was not ready for how it looked when he stepped off the elevator onto the Second Floor of the Residence. He and Harvey followed the sound of laughter from the elevator to the President's private Living Room.

As there were guests, two Secret Service agents flanked the door. Frank Adams was a massive man and the head of the President's Protection Detail. Beatrice Ann Belfour, commonly known as Beat, was a powerfully curved, much smaller, and supposedly even more dangerous version of her husband—though that was hard to imagine. It was generally agreed that the Presidential couple had the most dangerous team in or out of the military guarding them. Harvey joined them out in the Central Hall and Zack continued into the Living Room.

He nodded to the President and First Lady; nodded to Daniel and Alice as well before he caught sight of her.

Zack had expected Anne to still be wearing the silvered tie, which she was with the knot loose down to just above her breasts, but that was about all he recognized. Sometimes a man was lucky. He'd thought that many times since meeting Anne Darlington. And he'd thought it continuously as they'd romped back and forth through his hundred-and-twenty year old home. Still, it hadn't prepared him for this.

"Holy cow, Queen Anne. You're radiant."

"They did things to me," Anne flapped her hands helplessly. "I tried to stop them, but they overpowered me. Who knew that there were gangs of toughs inside dress shops and salons."

"Be quiet and just let me look," he knew she'd ignore his command. Except she did remain quiet. She also blushed and glared at him—both fiercely.

Her hair, that thick bounty of long hair he'd so enjoyed toying with last night, now shone as it spread over her shoulders. She had bought a dress, the kind that might have killed a lesser man. It wasn't sheer but it clung in amazing ways. Last night he'd seen the incredible conditioning of a life spent on a farm and riding horses. Tonight, her dress revealed it in whole new ways. He'd always thought himself unreasonably fortunate in the women he'd dated, but Anne Darlington was cut from a whole different cloth—in this case one of sky blue silk that complimented her dark blue eyes.

She'd retained her cowboy boots, though someone—he was sure it wasn't her—had thought to polish them to a brilliant mahogany shine. The skirt bloomed just above her knees, like she was ready for a country dance. A silver belt at her slim waist matched the tie, which was tucked under an over-wide starched collar that would have looked wrong on a woman with less strength of shoulder. The dress offered no cleavage, but instead was downright sinful in its accent of her shape.

"I want a picture of you in that for my shelf."

"I want a picture of your jaw hanging open," but she said it softly and offered him a smile of understanding. It was the same smile she'd offered as they stood before his photograph of the train set; one of deep sympathy and infinite understanding. Of course she'd understood the importance of his statement even if he hadn't when he'd said it. No one except his family and his trains appeared on that shelf. Yet still he wanted her there.

He moved over to hold her for just a moment. As he pulled her into his arms, Zack knew for certain that this wasn't going to be some typical DC affair, here and gone almost as fast as the news cycle. This was a woman he was going to hold onto for as long as possible.

# # #

Anne tried several times that evening to shoo Zack away, but wasn't having much luck with it. And the others weren't helping.

In the President's personal Living Room, she had ended up on one Chesterfield sofa with Zack while the President and First Lady Geneviève Matthews took the one opposite. Both couches were done in liquid brown leather. Daniel and Alice occupied a pair of wing-back armchairs. It was clear that the First Lady had made this room very masculine for her husband's sake. Anne wondered if he noticed quite how comfortable he was here.

The hand of the Christmas spirit had touched lightly here even though the family Christmas tree dominated one corner.

Presents were already accumulating under the pine branches which were covered in homey ornaments that could only have been gathered over decades of time. The glasses they used for eggnog had a holly pattern and the appetizer plates had that same pattern painted on the white china. But little else existed to mitigate the sheer maleness of the room.

They'd chatted about world events at a level that Anne was fairly sure she wasn't cleared for. Every now and then Daniel would start to raise some objection about her clearance level, and the President simply ran right over him. Geneviève, who Anne was still having problems with calling by her first name, didn't even bat an eye. After the second time, Alice nodded as if the President's choice made perfect sense. Zack had eyed her a time or two, so it wasn't just her imagination. Eventually only she and Daniel were twitching at the frankness and details revealed on certain topics. The President was welcoming her to a whole new level. On previous visits, the few times she saw Peter Matthews, conversations had turned instantly mundane in her presence. Not pointless or dumbed down, merely of no great import. Not so tonight.

The eggnog was spiked, which had gone straight to her head, but she managed not to wobble as they had adjourned to the Dining Room. She congratulated herself on making the transition comfortably as they crossed the Central Hall. Walking beside Alice and chatting about CIA analytical methods and how Alice had applied them to understanding why in the world Daniel had fallen for her, they approached the three agents who had moved down to the West Sitting Hall.

The Christmas elves had been here as well, with a much heavier hand. Great wreaths the size of a horse blanket hung along the walls. Woven streamers of red and green velvet draped the columns. It was elegant, tasteful, and decidedly merry.

The agents looked both in and out of place in the fine hall dressed in its Christmas attire. The three of them wore good quality dark suits and sat comfortably in nice period furniture.

She waved at Harvey who waved back. The other two were inspecting her with a degree of scrutiny that at first felt invasive it was so intense. Then she realized they were probably studying her for characteristic motion, potentially dangerous actions, or who knew what went on within a top agent's mind. Having finished whatever their inspection was, the huge man waved back in a friendly enough fashion. The woman still watched her carefully.

Then all three leapt to their feet as the President came into view behind her. Suddenly they looked like some Tom Cruise *Mission Impossible* team—dressed for a party and armed to kill.

"Dinner call," the President said in a friendly fashion. "I'll make sure trays get out to you."

"Thank you, sir. Very kind of you, Mr. President."

Anne glanced back as their party entered the Dining Room. The agents remained on alert, inspecting the long and empty hallway carefully before returning to their seats.

Maybe the transition to whatever inner circle she was being welcomed wasn't quite so comfortable. They were in the most heavily guarded home in America. They even had guards inside. How far away was the officer with the nuclear football? The medic in case the President choked or had a stroke? What about...

"What in blue hills am I doing here?" She whispered to Zack as he held out her chair.

"Being the first woman I've dated who has been invited to the First Family's table."

Anne was overwhelmed by several elements of that statement and went for the least scary one, "We're dating?" Though why she thought that was the *least* scary...

"Haven't you been watching the news?"

She sat and he took the chair close beside her. She'd hoped for a little more distance from the emotional power that Zack was wielding over her. But he was right and she'd known that from the moment she'd seen the look in his eyes as he'd arrived tonight. She was in so much trouble. No, she'd known it since they'd stood together in front of that childhood train photo. It was impossible that she somehow knew so much about him so soon, and yet it also felt perfectly right that she did.

They'd had a wonderful time last night, definitely the best sex she'd ever had. And Zachary Thomas wasn't only a powerful man, he was an immensely considerate lover. Either his past as an Air Force Captain or his present life as the Vice President gave him a certain tendency toward macho, but it was well balanced by his innate kindness. Her past experiences were with men who had smoother manners and gentler personalities; not Zachary's raw force of character.

In a dress—which made her feel exposed rather than beautiful—he'd looked at her as if she was indeed a queen—which made her feel beautiful rather than exposed. But seated side by side at the circular table, with their knees bumping against each other far more often than could be blamed on their relative positions, Zack was completely overloading her senses.

He was right, they were dating. She, Anne Darlington, was dating the Vice President of— Anne really wished she was a drinking woman.

The Dining Room also reflected a woman's touch. Christmas here was knick-knacks on the mantel: candy cane candles, a line of matryoshka wooden nesting dolls but in the form of reindeer, and an old steel frame with three aged brass bells just like the ones on the four-horse team they used to pull the farm's "sleigh." In Tennessee it had wheels rather than runners, but the Darlington farm had offered children free hayrides in it since the late-1800s.

They'd seated Daniel across the table which wasn't far enough—his constant hovering was making it hard to be herself; almost as much as wearing a dress. To her right sat Zack and Alice, who were still discussing climate change and world politics—apparently the Vice President had found the analyst he was looking for in Anne's sister-in-law. Alice rattled off project names and statistics as if this was her CIA specialty rather than North Korean and Chinese politics.

To her left sat the First Lady and President Matthews. Anne was a little surprised that they hadn't ended up man-woman the whole way around as was done at almost every formal dinner she'd ever attended or given. Sitting next to the First Lady was almost as daunting as sitting beside Zachary.

Geneviève was easily the most alarming woman Anne had ever met.

Of French-Vietnamese descent, not only was she a Director for the UNESCO World Heritage Convention, she notoriously had saved the President's life, married him, and given him a daughter—presently asleep with her nanny. As if that wasn't enough, the First Lady was a renowned beauty, as tall as the President with a statuesque figure, pale skin, and a lush fall of dark hair.

Why was Zack even looking at Anne when he could easily have his choice of similar smooth, urban beauties? Well, maybe not like Geneviève, but at least like Cornelia Day. Anne was so out of her league here that—

She shut down the thought and did what she could to survive the evening. Thankfully, her family entertained frequently and she'd known how to be social at a dinner table since before she'd learned to tie her shoelaces. If only Zachary hadn't hooked his foot around hers beneath the table. It forced her entire body to hum with anticipation throughout the meal.

Over dessert of sweet wine and braised pears, the First Lady winked at her, "This problem I know," she offered in her light French accent that only added to the perfection, unlike Anne's own Holly Hunter imitation making her sound all the more rural.

"What problem?"

"Oh dear. You are so in the beginnings that you do not even see. *Mais oui?* I have forgotten what that is like. I think that makes it a very good beginning. Very good. You must be calling me Genny from now on." Anne looked to Zack for some explanation, but he was talking to the President and Daniel about the Washington Redskins football team. Alice however, was leaning around Zack and watching the First Lady.

"Really?" Alice leaned further forward and looked carefully into Anne's face.

Anne almost reached for her napkin to wipe it clean. Or maybe she'd just hide behind the linen, do a magic trick and disappear.

"Oh!" Alice blinked in surprise. "I missed that," she spoke to Genny, then she flashed a huge smile at Anne.

"What?" Anne would have hissed it at Alice, but knew from experience that the best way to avoid attracting the attention of other people at the table was to speak perfectly normally.

True to form, there were two distinct conversations going on. The three men discussing a topic she'd be much more comfortable with, and the two women in deep cahoots over some thing or other that had Anne shifting nervously in her seat.

"Men," the First Lady clapped her hands together in a peremptory fashion. "Men, you are now going away. Watch one of your games or conquer the world to make your women safe."

The President leaned over to kiss his wife, Anne noted that it was far more than a casual act, then dutifully rose to his feet. Daniel—always too reserved—merely squeezed his wife's hand. Zachary rose, then leaned down to kiss her on top of the head. It was sweet and did nothing to calm her sudden nerves.

She looked at him, hoping that he'd see her expression begging him to take her away. But Zack didn't and merely proceeded on his way out the door with the others. Or perhaps he did and ignored it because no one argued with the First Lady.

Alice moved her teacup and then herself into Zack's seat. Now Anne was truly trapped.

# # #

"Frank," the President called out to the head of his Protection Detail as the three of them entered the West Sitting Hall. "Please tell me there's a game on."

In moments Frank and Harvey had followed them back to the Living Room. Beat headed in to check on the other women. And Zack wished Anne luck.

He was having trouble hiding his smile from the others. He'd seen Anne's panicked plea; couldn't have missed it from atop a Rocky Mountain peak. But she was just going to have learn the hard way—the same as he had—that Kim-Ly Geneviève Beauchamp Matthews was not as terrifying as she looked. Well, perhaps she was, but she was so awfully nice about it. However, the First Lady was not a woman to be denied and he wasn't about to try.

The President opened an armoire and revealed a large television. Frank dropped into one of the armchairs and began inspecting a football schedule on his phone.

Harvey looked at Zack as to whether he should stay and Zack could only shrug. Watching a friendly game with "the guys," he wasn't any more sure of the protocols than Harvey was. As VP, he'd been a common enough visitor on the second floor of the White House, but mostly as a part of social functions, which were a recent innovation.

First Lady Katherine Matthews, prior to her untimely death, had entertained without the President on the third floor where Daniel and Alice now lived. She and the President were only ever seen together when in public. The top floor had been Katherine's domain and, to the best of Zack's knowledge, the President still never went up there.

The White House had become a livelier and friendlier place with the arrival of Genny Matthews. She entertained more and it was as much through her as through Zack's own daily interactions with the President that he and Peter had become friends. But the President was very reserved in many ways—DC born and bred and perhaps overly self-conscious about his role. He only truly relaxed around his childhood friend turned helicopter pilot. Anne should be glad she wasn't facing Emily Beale; she was even more daunting than the First Lady.

# # #

Anne half rose to follow the men anyway, but when she turned, the female agent stood in the doorway. She was powerfully curved, and terribly imposing in her dark suit. A beautiful woman, but her standout feature was her eyes—they missed nothing.

They clearly didn't miss Anne's halfhearted attempt at beating a hasty retreat. She moved into a blocking position in the doorway. The agent was only a few inches taller than Anne, but Anne gave up any hopes of retreat when she noted how completely she blocked the doorway—she filled it more effectively than a woman twice her size.

"Beatrice," the First Lady spoke up without turning, "could you make us some tea, please? I would, but I fear that Anne will still need to decide in her mind that she is where she belongs. *Oui?*" Her position effectively blocked any escape to the left.

"Yes, ma'am." Beatrice offered a glare that told Anne she wasn't going anywhere, then turned for the small family kitchen. The main kitchen was downstairs from which their dinner had arrived via a dumbwaiter, to be served by stewards who ascended in the tiny elevator and had now departed.

"No, Genny," Alice blocked Anne's options to the right. "We don't need to worry. She's from Tennessee. Anne is too polite to run, even given the chance."

"Just…" Anne had to swallow against a dry throat, she really did need some tea. "Just try me. Give me an escape route and my next stop will be—"

"One Observatory Circle," Alice offered calmly. "While the Vice President might appreciate that, it is far too soon to appease him so easily."

Anne didn't want to appease him, she wanted to burrow up against his chest and hide from the two women facing her. Beatrice returned with a tray laden with rattling china, lemon, sugar, and milk. Make that three women facing her. Make it four and then she could be hiding from herself as well…which was exactly what she couldn't do. The First Lady was right; she couldn't run.

"Besides," Genny patted Anne's hand and she felt soothed despite herself, "it is time we came to know you just as it is time for Peter and Zachary to become more properly acquainted."

Anne was about to ask why now was any different than yesterday, but then decided she wouldn't like the answer.

"I looked for cookies, ma'am," Beatrice shrugged, "but—"

"The President has eaten them all, I know it is *très problématique*. He does this always, I must fight with tooth and nail for my share."

Anne recalled the box she'd stuffed into her pack before leaving Tennessee. "I brought Christmas cookies, ma'am. For Daniel, but I forgot to give them to him. They might be a little stale, but I can run up to my room and get them."

"Too distracted by a handsome Vice President, perhaps?" Alice teased.

"It's not fair that my favorite sister-in-law gets to tease me."

"As your only sister-in-law, I find the honor of 'favorite' unimpressive in that respect, but gladly accept it in all others. However, there's not a chance I'm letting you escape that easily. They're in your room?"

"On the night stand," Anne did her best to sound grouchy, but she liked Alice too much to put any heat behind it.

Alice left in pursuit of sugar and Beatrice returned to the kitchen at the kettle's shrill whistle.

The Dining Room was suddenly very quiet.

The First Lady reached out and took her hand. "My good friend, Anne. Do not be so afraid."

"I'm not actually afraid of any of you. Merely terribly humbled and completely out of my element."

"You are not scared, you are *terrifié!* But I agree that it is not of me or Daniel's Alice."

"I don't mind if she's afraid of me," Beatrice returned carrying a large snow-white teapot with black raven silhouettes soaring across the surface.

"Oh foof," the First Lady waved a dismissive hand. "You are not scary to the people you love."

Beatrice's easy shrug of acceptance also lifted her jacket enough to reveal the large handgun in the shoulder holster that rested against the side of her breast.

"It is," the First Lady returned her attention to Anne, "the man who has so touched your heart. *Mais oui?* He is what you cannot account for."

Anne did not like being so thoroughly transparent. However her likes and dislikes appeared to be of little consequence in this case. She toyed with Zack's tie a bit and felt a sense of comfort that only reinforced her growing feelings for him. She'd barely taken it off except to shower before dinner. Now she wished she'd run while she'd still had the chance.

"Here they are," Alice returned with the large box of homemade Christmas cookies.

That's when Anne remembered just what was in there. "Perhaps we should send down to the kitchen instead…" She reached for the box, but Alice held it away out of her reach as she sat down.

While Beatrice joined them, facing the door, and the First Lady poured, Anne tried to signal Alice about just what kind of cookies were in the box.

Alice merely smiled and began slitting the tape. After three years with Daniel she knew exactly what sort Anne always made for her brother.

# # #

"No games happing in the Eastern Conference, Mr. President," Frank announced.

"How about some Scrabble?"

Zack opened his mouth to say it wasn't really his game, but he'd be glad to take on the President—but Daniel cut him off.

"Don't! No, Mr. Vice President," Daniel began pulling beers out of a small mini-fridge. "Don't even think it. He and the First Lady would play at international levels if they could afford the three days for the World Championship. With their pseudonyms they anonymously rule the online Scrabble world."

The President was doing an impressive job of looking innocent and shocked. He was a skilled enough politician that Zack might have bought it…if he hadn't seen Frank Adams shaking his head warningly from close behind the President.

"How about Western Conference?" Zack went for the safe play.

"San Diego State is facing down Colorado State tonight," Frank announced.

"If they win," Harvey noted, "that will knock the Air Force Falcons completely out of the running after the whupping they took from Stanford."

"Hey," Zack did his best to glare at his agent. "I thought you were supposed to defend me?"

"Only from bad guys, Mr. Vice President," Harvey answered easily. "Bad teams, I've got no help for you."

"They weren't bad. They just…" It was a losing argument anyway, because…

"…got their butts kicked," the President wasn't being helpful either.

"I could have outrun those guys," Harvey muttered, "and I'm not talking about back in the day."

To tease Zack, Anne had rooted for Stanford during the game when they'd watched it last night. Last night? Had it been so recently? He tried counting back the days, but it didn't work. He reached two and that was as far as it went. The concert at the Conservatory and last night. He'd never, well, not since his Air Force days, slept with a woman on their second date.

Last night he may not have slept much, but he'd certainly made love to Anne Darlington. As memorable as those moments had been, they were not the highlights that came first to mind. Much more strongly he remembered her lying in his arms on the Library couch wearing only his tie and one of his dress shirts unbuttoned, curled up together beneath a blanket and content to just watch the game as if they'd done it a thousand nights before.

But most of all, he remembered when she had turned from his photo to look at him. *I think Mr. Vice President that it is dangerous for two such lonely people to stand here in such silence.*

He had been raised beneath a shroud of impenetrable silence. He had escaped and filled his world with his own achievements: Air Force, state Senate, Governor, and Vice President. But Anne had seen past that so effortlessly. She'd also seen the boy he'd thought was carefully hidden—so deep that Zack himself only saw him on rare and particularly lonely nights.

A bright laugh sounded from across the hall just as Frank turned up the volume on the television.

"Tonight," one of the announcers spoke snidely as if he knew the Vice President had just tuned in, "San Diego is expected to trounce Colorado State with a projected sixteen point spread and secure their place in the playoffs."

Bad news all around.

# # #

When they opened the cookie box, sharp ginger and sweet sugar overwhelmed the scent of the chamomile tea until it was thick in the Dining Room. Anne wanted to hide her head in shame as the other three women howled with laughter over the cookies. Even Beatrice's serious demeanor had cracked as the first of "Anne's Specials"—as her Christmas cutout cookies were known in the family—were revealed.

Alice picked up a decidedly sneaky looking elf spiking Santa's eggnog. That wasn't too bad.

Beatrice's selection was a pair of gingerbread reindeer lying together as if exhausted by sex. A little too reminiscent of Anne's own position in Zack's arms last night.

Then the First Lady reached into the box and unearthed Mr. and Mrs. Claus. Santa was bent down as if peeking under his wife's red royal icing dress complete with white trim.

The three of them were laughing and comparing the cookies.

Anne resisted hanging her head, "I made them to embarrass Daniel, not me."

"And how is that working for you?" Alice bit off the sly elf's head.

"About as well as usual," Anne suddenly felt very sad. Nothing was going the way she'd planned this holiday season. She'd always enjoyed Christmas, it was a wonderful time on farm, but this time all she felt was misery.

"She needs a cookie," Beatrice nudged the box across the table.

Anne reached in without looking. For a moment she didn't even remember making this cookie, but it had her trademark style. And then she remembered the painstaking decorations she'd done. Gingerboy and gingergirl stood hip to hip with their arms around each other's waist. She'd decorated it to be Alice and Daniel; after all, the box had been intended for them. It was the one sweet cookie in a box of questionable elves and sated reindeer.

She tried to hand the cookie over to Alice, "You should save this one, I made it of the two of you."

Alice studied it, but didn't take it from her. "That doesn't look like me, that looks like you."

"No it doesn't," but even as she said it, Anne was studying the cookie. The gingergirl didn't have the curly brunette mop that always looked so cute on Alice, instead she had long blond hair like Anne's own. Why had she done that? And the gingerboy didn't look like Daniel, but instead was mostly faceless with non-descript hair.

Geneviève leaned in closely and rested a hand on Anne's shoulder. "Now that you know what your true love looks like, you can finish this cookie and make it *idéal!*"

It would take only the tiniest bit of royal icing to draw in Zack's dark hair and beard, his warm brown eyes would be hard to match for they were so alive, and of course a silver tie, for she would always think of him in it. Then it would be—

"My what?" The First Lady's words had finally sunk in like a hammer blow.

"Twelve seconds," Alice looked up from her watch. "You have an impressive reaction time, sister. Slow on the uptake, but your recovery time was far better than mine. When Emily told me that I loved Daniel, I heard her sooner, but it was at least a minute and a glass of wine about so large," she held her palms way apart, "before I was able to respond."

"My grandmother," Genny said with a happy smile and a soft sigh. "On our farm in Vietnam while the President waited in the kitchen and my sister Jacqui—who is so very shameless—flirted with him. Gram said I already knew who was inside of my heart and I simply decided she was right because Gram always is."

They all turned to Beatrice. She grimaced before biting off one of the reindeer's heads and rinsing it down with some tea, "Frank told me. I had to go and help invade Panama before I figured out he was right."

Then they all turned back to Anne.

She bit off the gingerboy's and then the gingergirl's heads, eliciting a grin from Beatrice, then replied with her mouth still full, "I still don't know squat."

They all laughed, but Genny's smile told her that she wasn't fooling anyone, not even herself.

How could she *not* love the lonely boy turned into the magnificent man?

Chapter 5

*W*hat do you mean you have to go?"

The days flew by as Anne settled into a lovely routine at One Observatory Circle. Her dinner with the First Family had been leaked by the First Lady's press office and duly noted by the gossip columns. The media's tone had shifted immediately from "Who is this tramp?" to "Is the nation's most eligible bachelor finally off the market?" An elegant move by an elegant First Lady.

As the spotlight shifted to the Darlingtons, Ma had swung into action. She'd been very pleased for Anne—other than being a little huffy about finding out through the media rather than directly from her daughter. Anne had called her as soon as the news broke, but CNN had beat her call to Tennessee. There was little the two of them hadn't shared over the years and her mother had been as enthusiastic as her new female friends had been after dinner that night.

Mary Annette Darlington also was the advertising and marketing specialist of the family. By day three of Anne's affair with the Vice President, the Darlington Estate web site had shifted in tone. Family history press packets appeared, tracing their roots back to Colonial times, as did individual profiles—Anne's cast her in an uncomfortably heroic light. She couldn't quite put her finger on it, for all of Ma Darlington's facts were true, but they made Anne sound like so much more than she knew she was.

A week passed, and most of a second, but Cornelia Day had become no more pleasant than at their first meeting. Anne had developed some patience with her constant animosity. After all, protecting the Vice President was a concern they shared. But that one common shared goal certainly wasn't enough to warrant a peace accord.

"Thanks, Jim," Zack said to the Navy steward who was serving them breakfast. Short stack with coffee for her, tall stack with sausage, bacon, orange juice, and coffee for him.

"Thank you, James," she echoed, but her heart wasn't in it this morning.

The sunlight, for a century so carefully measured and timed by the Naval Observatory, shone down out of a clear blue sky oblivious that the USNO now supplied the nation's time markers from an atomic clock, rather than a solar sighting.

Zack had taken her to see it one evening, a short and very chilly walk across the campus. It consisted of a dozen racks of non-descript computer equipment and a sign that said "USNO Master Clock" in bright red electronic letters. Another displayed the official time out to the kazillionths of a second. They'd also walked through the largest astronomical library in the US which was impressive and almost utterly meaningless. She'd gotten to peek through a twenty-six-inch refractor telescope, which was oddly forty-feet long and showed startling objects. Clearly the technicians were used to looking at far more strange and esoteric things than a Horsehead Nebula, so she had not delayed them long.

Zack's Dining Room at One Observatory Circle had a long formal walnut table with elegant chairs. It could easily seat a dozen, instead the two of them sat across from each other at one end. One of the stewards, probably Sharelle for she had the best eye, had placed the flowers so that the table didn't look empty, but rather their part of it was simply smaller. The fire snapped warm and bright in the fireplace, a simple garland draped over the mantelpiece. The room had none of the homey touches that the First Lady had placed about the White House Residence.

Despite spending nights at the heart of American national timekeeping, Anne rarely cared what time it was more accurately than morning versus afternoon. But now their time together was growing short and she was discovering that she cared very much.

"When?"

"I fly out to Italy this evening."

"Tonight?" Anne's heart stopped along with her fork halfway from plate to mouth.

"The Climate Conference at Courmayeur. I've been working on it all week," he was looking at her in a slightly bemused way.

"Courmayeur." By sheer force of will, Anne managed to get her fork underway again and placed the first bite of pancake in her mouth. She chewed because something was there, not because she could taste it. She'd heard, she knew, but it simply hadn't impinged on her world until this moment.

"Italy. We've grown tired of the idiot rioters both for and against the environment. Rather than some major city, we're going to meet very quietly in a tiny Italian resort."

"You're leaving for Italy this evening." And what was she supposed to do? For an entire, glorious ten days, she'd done absolutely no thinking. All she'd allowed herself to do was feel.

The days had been spent touring about DC, more at the whim of the agent the Secret Service had assigned to guarding her than her own. Detra was a overtly positive, buxom blond who was immensely entertaining.

"You're my first protectee you know. Solo I mean. I've been in the Protection Detail for over a year, an agent for three years since I qualified. So you shouldn't feel worried about my being some beginner. I haven't lost anyone yet," she barely slowed down for a perky smile filled with perfect teeth. "What do you mean you've never seen the Declaration? Your file said that you were D.A.R. One of your direct relatives signed."

Her mother was from Georgia which had been one of the original states, and had brought her membership as a Daughter of the American Revolution across state lines to Johnny Darlington's farm, along with her accent. No one could ever tell whether mother or daughter had answered the phone, not even Daniel, which had led to some spectacular opportunities to give him lectures throughout the years.

"That's huge," Detra had proclaimed. "Let's go find it!" And they'd be off.

Evenings had been spent with Zack. She'd dined twice more at the White House, once with the First Family and once with just Daniel, Alice, and Zack in the upstairs kitchen. They'd attended a holiday concert of Handel's *Messiah* in the National Cathedral. It was one of the most moving things she ever heard; the space itself was beautiful enough to be a religious experience even without the music.

And there'd been a "strictly social" dinner at the Speaker's house in Georgetown. Even though Zack and the Speaker were from different parties, it was clear they were quite good friends. And the Speaker's wife had made no attempt to disguise her joy at the social coup of being the first to host Anne Darlington.

Anne had been to far too many formal dinners to disappoint and had forced herself to purchase a second dress for the occasion.

Now, whether her reputation thrived or crashed and burned, Mrs. Speaker would gain bragging rights in either direction. Ultimately, despite the circumstances, she'd found herself liking the Speaker's wife.

That had left only a few evenings at One Observatory Circle. The second night she'd worried about how to discretely move her meager belongings from the White House to the Vice President's without imposing. Zack had solved that by simply asking if she wanted to pack her bags after the First Family's dinner.

It was the nights that were so new to her. They soon felt as if she'd never been anywhere else. Anne had never lived with a man before. Stayed with them on occasion, but there was no doubt that she and the Vice President were living together. When you were handing off the toothpaste tube while brushing your teeth together in the same bathroom, there was no avoiding the fact.

And tonight she'd be living…where?

"I was rather hoping you could come with me, unless you have somewhere else you have to be."

"Italy?" Anne knew she was being thick headed, but couldn't seem to shake it off. She'd had her morning coffee. Goodness, she'd had amazing wake-up sex and a beautiful man to scrub her back in the shower, though he'd insisted on washing her hair each morning which took forever to dry. But he enjoyed it so much, she hadn't had the heart to use a shower cap.

Still, her mind was having trouble keeping up with the new play that had just been called. "Italy," she repeated once more.

"Uh-huh," Zack was clearly enjoying the moment, grinning at her over a sip of his orange juice.

She took a deep breath and held it. Not that she was all that great at doing so for very long, but she'd always told herself that if you couldn't make a decision in the amount of time she could hold her breath, then it wasn't time to make it.

Did she want to be with Zack? More than any man in her past…or that she could imagine in her future, but she couldn't hold her breath long enough to think out the consequences of that one.

Did she want to travel to Italy? She loved Italy.

Did she want to travel to Italy with the Vice President? That answer was far less clear.

She could see in his eyes that there was more than merely the travel. It was the quiet of the man facing the boy's rail yard picture.

If she traveled with him, she would be labeled "mistress." They both knew that.

If she traveled with him, it would mean far more was happening between them than an incredibly pleasant affair. It meant they were lovers who were…

Anne was running out of air. She needed time on that last point but that quiet in his eyes worried her. She didn't want to hurt Zack's feelings either. To cover the small gasp to refill her aching lungs, she reached out with a fork and snagged one of his link sausages and bit off the end.

"Well, Mr. Vice President," even in the most intimate moments, she had yet to wholly drop the honorific, "that doesn't strike me as *much* closer to the North Pole."

"Actually, Expedition Leader, Courmayeur is well north of DC. I checked for you. It is almost four hundred miles farther north."

"So is the state of Maine. I'll have to inspect my expedition supplies and get back to you." She could see the hurt on his features and she reached across to take his hand for a moment.

He squeezed it very hard as if holding on for dear life.

She felt much the same way. "Just give me a few hours. I remember you mentioning this, but I never thought I'd go along."

He nodded and managed to dredge up an easy smile for her, but she could see that it cost him to do so. She almost said yes right then, but that was the happy mistress' answer, not the lovers'. And definitely not the—

Anne chopped off that thought hard, though it wasn't far away. If she was ever going to spend her life with a man, it would be someone like Zachary Thomas. Just like him. But she didn't want merely to be some man's wife no matter who he was.

She did her best to return his smile and could only hope that he didn't see what it cost her.

# # #

They rode to the White House together in silence, where Cornelia eyed her coolly as the Vice President disappeared into his first meeting. Every single agency in DC wanted input on what he was going to say at the upcoming conference.

When the US had announced that they were sending the VP, it had forced all of the other countries attending to step up their game. Second- or third-level department heads were being replaced by vice-ministers, and even undersecretaries were completely passé. Now it would be a conference of people who could actually make decisions.

Anne didn't know why she was hesitating here in Zack's outer office.

Apparently Cornelia didn't either. She slowly melted from cold to curious, without quite looking up from her desk.

Anne kept looking over her shoulder, as it felt like there was another person in the room. In a way, there was. Someone had decorated the VP's office into a full Victorian-style Christmas. It was the happy-ever-after of Scrooge; the party that Mr. Fezziwig would have thrown in Scrooge's youth. Garlands and a wreath sported bows in period fabrics. Some fine weavings—clearly museum pieces—had been hung on the walls. And a girl-mannequin in full attire stood looking out the window at the EEOB across the street. She was complete with a Christmas basket and, Anne peeked beneath the bright cloth, a—she tapped it with a fingernail—plastic figgy pudding.

Beyond the window, another light snow was falling on DC. Mid-December had not eased off from the chill and bluster that had begun the month which still made the parka her coat of choice.

"Is there something I can do for you, Ms. Darlington?" Cornelia was as polite as could be, a dangerous sound. How little would it take for her to maneuver Anne's reputation right into the mud or… But she hadn't. Instead she had kept the Vice President right on schedule and prepared him for the upcoming trip.

"Was it your idea?" Anne wasn't quite sure where the question had come from.

"The Victorian décor? No way." It was the one hint Anne had heard of her California background—an accent and speech pattern otherwise very well hidden.

"No. Sending the Vice President to the climate conference. It's brilliant actually," and it was more brilliant each time she thought about it.

"No. It was the Vice President's. Many have labeled it political as the President is already well into his second term, but he doesn't care about how it looks. He cares about the results." Cornelia's voice had once again grown haughty.

But Anne could only nod. That fit the man she knew. The Coloradan who had complained about the failing snow on the ski areas in the same breath as the raging wildfires across his home state and others. President. Somehow she hadn't thought about Zachary Thomas being the next obvious candidate. An immensely popular one even without the climate conference.

"Sorry," Cornelia offered in a contrite voice. "You bring out the nasty in me. I don't even know why."

Anne looked at her in surprise. "I thought that was obvious. Either you love him yourself or you are convinced that I'm not good enough for him. You won't find me arguing on either point."

"You are wrong. You are very good for him. *That* is the problem."

Anne decided that sitting down would be a good idea at that moment. Suddenly she was the shortest one in the room, both the mannequin and the seated Cornelia towered above her. "How is that a problem?"

Cornelia didn't fuss with her pen or straighten her notepad. Instead she simply folded her hands atop her desk and looked at Anne with a forthrightness unbecoming to a Southerner.

"Already he depends on you. I often hear him discussing ideas in meetings that are unusual for him. You make a thoughtful man think even more deeply."

Anne could only blink in surprise. She and Zack often spoke about whatever he was reading; over a meal, riding in the motorcade, or curled up together. It gave them something to talk about other than themselves. But that she was affecting his decisions was another new idea in an already busy morning.

"When I joined him, I had a terrible crush on him. I was fresh out of college at twenty—three year program; an overachiever and valedictorian like yourself. But he was already thirty. I knew I had a choice: take a chance that he would have me and perhaps ruin his career with my youth, or work for a man I respect immensely. I chose the latter."

Anne still was unable to move under the steady weight of Cornelia's gaze.

"You are much nearer his age and I can see how you are changing him for the better. He is different with you than any other woman and if you suddenly decide to go, the effect could be devastating—not only on the news cycle, but on him as well. He's never taken anyone to see the Conservatory for Christmas before. It is something that he does every year and for some reason it is very private to him. Yet he took you. I don't know whether or not to trust you, Ms. Darlington."

Anne knew the reason behind Zack's privacy and once again hurt for the lonely boy alone each Christmas, journeying to watch the model trains. She was also in awe that he had shared it with her. Had she returned the favor? Anne had shared her body and her joy with him, but she hadn't shared but a glimpse of her own inner turmoil. It had taken her a decade of chafing at the bit before she'd known that the farm was no longer for her. She had come to DC more as a declaration to herself than to Daniel that she was moving on.

But she didn't know to where.

"Would it make you feel any better, Ms. Day, that I don't trust myself either?"

She tipped her head in thought, a long elegant gesture. For the first time Anne could see the nerves behind the careful façade. Cornelia presented the DC shark to the world, but there was someone softer inside and it made Anne feel more kindly toward her.

"I'll make you a deal, Cornelia."

The woman arched a single eyebrow at her.

"I'll make sure that you're the third to know if I turn out to be trustworthy, next in line after the Vice President."

"And who before that?" her tone turned suspicious.

"Me."

Cornelia actually laughed, a wholly unexpected sound that lightened her face. For an instant a much younger girl showed through. She reached across the desk and offered a firm handclasp which Anne returned in surprise.

"I may like you yet, Ms. Darlington."

"The surprise is mutual, Ms. Day." Anne suspected they could even become friends, which was an even greater shock. Anne had plenty of friends back in Tennessee, but they were more for socializing with. Aside from her mother—who she'd discovered to be a wonderful and thoughtful woman once they'd both survived Anne's terrible teens—Anne had enjoyed more heart-to-hearts with astonishing women in the last week than in the prior decade.

"Will we be seeing you on the plane, Ms. Darlington?"

"Anne. And I don't know yet. I'd best go talk to my brother and see if he can help me decide."

"He left for the Hill an hour ago. He's not expected back until after it would be time to depart for the airport. Would you like me to try and reach him for you?"

Anne shook her head. She didn't know if he'd be of help anyway, but her options were running a tad bit thin. She certainly wasn't going to talk to the President about the implications of her sex life with his VP.

Cornelia's phone rang.

Anne waved for her to take it, "I'll go wander the halls and see what inspiration strikes."

"Good luck," Cornelia mouthed as she lifted the phone. It looked as if she meant it.

# # #

"The CIA analyst is here for your next meeting, Mr. Vice President."

Zack waved a hand for Cornelia to send him in without looking up from his notes. "Find out what they'd like for lunch and order two of them, would you?"

"Peasant under glass. Make it a cute one."

Zack glanced up to see Alice Darlington grinning at him. "I've been following up on the conversations we had last week, so they sent me to brief you." She plummeted into the chair across his desk in a way that he was learning was a Darlington-woman trademark—native-born or married-in. Alice wore a red cardigan with a brown moose knit in above her left breast. Knitted snow slipped down from the white collar in tiny stitches of white, some landing on the moose's back and antlers. She wore a matching knit hat that did little to control the brown curls of her hair.

"If you can't find a cute peasant, I'll take a turkey on rye and a Coke. Thanks, Cornelia."

His assistant disappeared.

Zack looked down at the thick files Alice was holding and did his best not to wince. What he wanted to do was track down Anne and talk her into going with him, hours had gone by and he still hadn't heard her decision about Italy. Instead, he'd focus on climate change and pay attention to the present. "Please tell me there's a short version to those files."

Alice had shed her hat so her cheerful nod swirled dark hair over her green eyes. "No, wait, these are the short version."

Zack gave a dutiful groan and hoped she was teasing.

"Or we can talk about my sister-in-law."

He glanced at the door, saw that Cornelia had considerately closed it, and he turned once more to face Alice. Did he dare?

Was it cheating to talk to one woman about another? Or even worse, discussing Daniel's sister with his wife? He decided that he didn't care.

"I'd like that."

"Good! Eleven days you've been playing house together, if you count the first night before she moved in as well. Please tell me you have done more than had sex with her."

Zack had to blink hard to catch up with the conversation.

"Of course I have. We've eaten, slept, showered, watched football. A wide variety of other activities."

"So, playing house with the pretty lady. But what about *her?*"

"What about her?" One of his specialties was his ability to anticipate and even control the conversation. He'd crossed from the Colorado Senate into the Governorship in only three years. He'd stopped strikes, proposed and passed wildfire legislation, even managed to lead migrant workers and union leaders to the same table and hammered out accords between them. Keeping ahead of Alice Darlington was being another challenge entirely; he wasn't even sure what the conversation was.

Alice thumped the stack of files down on his desk, crossed her arms, and flipped enough hair aside to glare at him with one eye. "You do know why she came to Washington DC, don't you? And before you answer that, no, it had nothing to do with you."

Zack had lost sight of that. He thought back to that first meeting in Daniel's office. She'd been...sad. She hid it well beneath that wall of easy humor, but the sadness had been there. And lonely.

"Two such lonely people," she'd said.

Somehow, this beautiful charismatic woman thought she was alone in the world. He'd watched her laughing with Alice, the First Lady, and even the agents, Beatrice and Detra. He'd seen her tease her brother until the Chief of Staff was at a complete loss for what to do next—and Daniel *always* knew what to do next.

"Ah, the light goes on!" Alice pointed to the ceiling as if she controlled the sun itself.

Anne had come to tell Daniel she was done with the family farm, but never a word about what came next. They were practically living together and Zack suddenly understood just how little he knew about her. Her hesitation at breakfast this morning suddenly made perfect sense, as if she was finding her way in the dark—one step at a time. And he had left her alone on her journey.

"I have to go find her," he pushed to his feet just as Cornelia opened the office door carrying a lunch tray set up for two.

"She's with the First Lady, Mr. Vice President," Cornelia set the tray down and looked at him levelly. The anger and mistrust that had simmered all week and flared every time Anne was mentioned had disappeared. Instead…

Zack slowly lowered himself back into his chair as the two women watched him.

"Well, I wouldn't presume to interrupt her there." At his nod, Cornelia withdrew, but he suddenly wondered who's side she was on. He pulled over a sandwich and a bag of chips. "Let's see what's in those files, Alice."

"As you wish, Mr. Vice President," and she opened the first one.

# # #

Anne had wandered for much of the morning. Detra had caught her mood and faded into the background. Anne's badge gained her admittance to much of the complex and she let the ebb and flow of the Christmas tide carry her along. The West Wing was a hive of activity and purposefulness that rapidly drove her toward the Residence. She discovered the China Room and the Map Room, but neither held her attention.

She spent a while sitting with the main White House Christmas tree in the Blue Room. It was a peaceful corner, well out of everyone's way. The eighteen-foot blue spruce was even bigger than the farm's traditional monster. The White House had elicited ornaments from fifth-grade classes in every state capital.

Tens of thousands of white balls had been sent out and the best of each school had been chosen to travel to DC. Hundreds of red-nosed reindeer, green-clad elves (who weren't spiking Santa's eggnog), and cheery Santas adorned the tree. Some bore the state fish or bird; it was a very merry tree.

"What if?" she asked the tree. It was a fairly obvious question.

What if she and Zack became a couple?

What if he was elected President at the end of Peter Matthew's second term?

Would she be sitting here some few years in the future and the grandest achievement of her year would be the theme of a White House Christmas tree? She'd rather be back on the farm if that was the case. There, at least, she knew what was needed and expected of the only Darlington daughter. The farm needed her, or could at least make good use of her, but she didn't need or want the farm.

She—

"Look!"

Anne glanced over to see a tour was entering the room. Cameras out, snapping pictures. Except they weren't looking at the tree, nor photographing it.

"It's that woman." "The Vice President's girlfriend." "Oh, she's so much prettier in real life." "Can I get your picture with us?" "Can I—"

Anne put on her best happy face, and retreated as quickly as possible without being rude. Down the Central Hall. Past the Vermeil Room and the Library. She almost ducked into the latter, but the open doors and cloth ropes indicated that tours would invade there as well.

The double doors at the end of the hall plunged her into yet another crowd forming up.

"It's the Visitor's Lobby," Detra had magically appeared at her elbow and Anne almost cried out in relief. "We need to get you out of here. Let's go see the Kennedy Garden." And with a casual looping of her arm through Anne's they were out into the freezing cold and fluttering snow even as people were calling her name. She'd never even had a chance to see the decorations.

"You're kidding me," her teeth were chattering before they'd gone five steps. Her parka was hanging in Daniel's outer office back in the West Wing.

"Sorry, best I have on short notice."

The rose bushes had been pruned back to little more than twigs rising from the soil. The grass was hidden beneath snowy paths. A dozen fake reindeer, in full harness, were standing in the central path of garden. One of the two lead reindeer was leaning forward as if to nibble a rose bush. A mighty sleigh filled with giant bags overflowing with ornaments were at the far end of the path.

"At least you're wearing boots," Detra commented.

Anne looked down at the agent's shoes, barely as high as the snow and definitely not up to making the crossing with dry feet. Anne felt bad for saying anything.

In moments, they were through the garden and an agent had a door open into the East Wing. Anne ducked inside and did her best to suppress her next shiver.

"Might I suggest a coat next time you want to visit the gardens in mid-December, ma'am."

She looked up and recognized Beatrice who was clearly amused by the situation.

Anne had to admit that it was hard not to be. "Seen a lot of protectees running scared?"

Beatrice and Detra both nodded, "From crowds of tourists? All the time."

Anne turned to her agent who was trying to be circumspect about knocking the snow out of her shoes. "Thank you, Detra."

"My pleasure, ma'am."

Then Anne figured out the implications of Beatrice's presence. The East Wing was the First Lady's domain and if the head of her Protection Detail was here, so was the First Lady.

Well, with Daniel on the Hill and Alice locked away in some cloister out at CIA headquarters in Langley, she was down to two options. She could call Ma and have a nice whine together; that would cheer her up but probably move her no closer to an answer. Or she could see if the First Lady was available. Anne remembered Geneviève's easy kindness every time they'd met, but that wasn't enough to tip the scale in favor of approaching the daunting First Lady. However, her comment to Anne the first time they were alone together came to mind. "Do not be afraid."

She was and she didn't like it.

Maybe Genny Matthews—she no longer thought of her as Geneviève nor the First Lady, but Genny—was the woman she *needed* to talk to.

"I don't suppose that…" No, she must be as busily scheduled as the President.

"She has just ordered lunch," Beatrice informed her. "She is part French and does not believe in working through lunches. Let me see if she's available. I can easily make the order for two."

Moments later, Anne was being escorted up the stairs and into the second floor of the East Wing. Down a long corridor that was little more than a blur of door signs: Calligraphers Office, The Office of the Social Secretary, Social Media Director, Event Coordinator. She was shown into the First Lady's office without even a pause to catch her breath; which was just as well as it also precluded any chance to second guess herself.

Like Daniel's, it had a southwest corner exposure. Except it overlooked the Kennedy Gardens with its plastic reindeer, the Residence, and the White House grounds rather than West Executive Avenue and the Executive Office Building.

Like Daniel's—in a crowded building where space was at a premium and size denoted importance—it was a large and comfortable space.

Unlike Daniel's it was immaculate, intensely feminine, and had a communications center that looked as if it could run a war.

Chapter 6

*W*hat in the world do you do here? Fly the space shuttle?"

"*Bonjour,* my dear Anne," Genny turned from her desk, which faced the view, and rose to greet Anne. Her dress of pale rose linen looked both practical and fashionable. Her easy hug was thoughtlessly welcoming, simply a natural extension of Genny's warmth. "*Non.* But at times I think that perhaps I could have while it still flew. Such fine technology as this still does not limit the nonsense that it can convey. The many countries of the UN must talk and talk and talk before they can make even the smallest decision."

It was easy to forget that the First Lady was also the UN "Ambassador" for the UNESCO World Heritage Convention. She was the chief peacekeeper and dealmaker for the thousand World Heritage sites and the hundreds under consideration. No wonder she needed so much conferencing equipment. There was little that couldn't be done at the Darlington's farm with a phone or a tactfully worded e-mail; this was a very different-colored horse.

Genny waved her to a small side table. Unlike the monster at the Vice President's residence, this table could seat only four, six in a pinch. However like Zachary's home it lacked…

"What happened to Christmas?" All Anne could pick out was a two-foot tall Christmas tree standing on a low side table and a small quilt of a polar bear staring upward at a starry sky.

"The French and the Vietnamese are far more understated than Americans about the season. I decorate the Residence for Peter and for the photographers. I decorate my office for myself. For us, the season is about sharing and food."

And as lunch was delivered, Anne knew that she'd be hard-pressed to argue. A winter minestrone with thick slices of fresh-baked sourdough. A small cup of yogurt and melon drizzled with honey accompanied by small selection of cookies that were, thankfully, White House chef elegant rather than Anne Darlington outrageous.

"You have reached the problem," Genny was the first to break the silence of good food.

She had. Apparently far too obviously.

"We will ignore that while we eat. Instead, I will speak of what *I* am troubled by, so that you may stop worrying for a time." And Genny began discussing the challenges of World Heritage site selection: limited funds, uncooperative governments, rampant poaching in the nature reserves, and no actual authority to implement solutions. "Everything it is a negotiation."

"Everything everywhere," Anne agreed.

The Darlington Estate had grown to encompass dozens of different efforts. Everything from horse breeding—they specialized in the Tennessee Walkers, tall majestic animals—to a fine dining restaurant with a menu almost wholly produced on the farm. Flour was one of the few things that was brought in from outside; honey or sorghum was used for sweetenings and wine was "imported" from the next valley over. There was an educational center for Slow Food and local farming techniques. In nearby Johnson City there was even a campaign center for lobbying Congress regarding non-GMO products, hazards of mono-culture farming, and the like. A hundred projects with a thousand demands.

"Yes, it is just so," Genny waved a hand toward the communication center behind her. "I must decide if the Pacific Island nations that are likely to be submerged by global warming have a higher claim to recognition than the primeval beech forests of the Ukraine. Both will be gone without UNESCO protection. Both may be gone even if it is granted. How am I supposed to make these kinds of decisions? *Je ne sais pas.*"

A pleasant hour flew by as she and Genny discussed different ways to approach that problem and others. Over a second cup of tea and the chocolate-dipped macaroons, Genny nodded as if reaching some decision.

"Hmm?" Anne asked as she debated whether to stop or to try a chocolate sable cookie. Go for it.

"You are as good at this as I thought you would be," the First Lady abstained from another cookie.

"As good at what?" Anne bit down and, at her intentionally amplified yummy sound, Genny Matthews caved and took one as well.

"I know the site buildings and the regional history. But I know little of nature. On our farm in Vietnam we only grow coffee and what food we can for ourselves, but I never care for that just as you do not care for your farm."

"No. Wait. I—" At Genny's raised hand Anne sputtered to a stop.

"I do not say that you do not love it or do not wish it well protected, but you wish someone else to do it and not you. I know this feeling as much as you do."

"Right down to the heels of my boots."

"That is why I come to work for the UN. That is how I met your President. I try to force him to fix a problem with an ancient temple that Cambodia and Thailand fight over. I did not think he is going to marry me for seeking his aid."

"What are you saying?"

"I am saying that you care very deeply about the land, about any land. You do not care so much for the tending, but your heart has no question about the land. While you are in Italy, you must look at Mont Blanc Massif. When you return from Italy, we will talk of what you see."

"Italy?" Anne almost lost her china teacup at the sharp veer in the conversation's direction. "I still don't know if I'm going. That's actually what I wanted to talk to—"

"Piff! Of course you are going to Italy. It is so romantic a place. You will see Courmayeur. You will eat fine food in a tiny *ristorante*. You will make passionate love in an Italian villa."

"But…" Anne didn't even know where to begin. "But…I don't want to hurt Zachary's—the Vice President's reputation. The media will look at me and—"

"I am a French-Vietnamese woman. I fall in love with your President after his very popular first wife is dead—though the stories I hear about her…" Genny shivered as if all of her office windows were suddenly open to the December storm wrapping its fist around DC. "You are American woman in love with an American man; your states are as close together as two pea vines compared to my country and Peter's. This makes it much less of a trouble. Go! Enjoy Italy."

And once again, events swept out of Anne's control.

The UNESCO World Heritage Ambassador to the UN assembly turned back to her work. Detra gathered her up in the East Wing hall and handed over her parka. In moments she was down through the tunnel underneath East Executive Avenue and into the garage beneath the Treasury Building. The black SUV slid out into DC traffic and a thick snowfall.

"Where are we going?" Anne gathered some thread of common sense as they passed the Jefferson Memorial and turned east. "Isn't the Vice President's house that way?"

Detra nodded affably. "It is. Nothing wrong your sense of direction."

"But—"

"Andrews Field is this way. Air Force Two is just warming up on the tarmac. The Vice President is running behind."

"But—" Anne tried again.

"One of the Navy stewards packed your clothes and other belongings. They're right behind you."

Anne twisted around to see her knapsack and the clothes bag with her two dresses. Not a single piece of it was appropriate for where she was going; Italian women always dressed well and she'd come to DC with little more than jeans and turtlenecks. Of course, there was nowhere to buy fashionable clothes quite like Italy.

The last "but" she could think of, which was also the first, had been answered by Genny Matthews, the woman who loved the President.

Was Anne herself *in love?* Genny had pointed it out at that first dinner as if it had been a neon sign blazing on Anne's forehead. Cornelia Day seemed to think so as well. It was getting hard to deny, so she supposed she was. That sounded like a lame revelation.

"In love" was supposed to have lightning bolts, choirs of angels, and hard-bodied men. Okay, perhaps it did have the first and last of those, but where was the heavenly choir? It was the right season after all. She'd never imagined that love would arrive like a favorite pair of slippers, but it did fit ever so fine.

So, no longer a question, she was in love. In love with Zachary Thomas. She tested it as they zipped onto the field. The thought had a warm, cozy, fireside feel to it and was as natural as their lovemaking.

The next question: what was she going to do about it? Not thinking had gotten her this far and she considered sticking with that plan of action.

No.

It was time to stop drifting, she checked her mental calendar. The Thanksgiving banquet had been twenty days ago. She'd been living at One Observation Circle for the last eleven; living with someone—which should not be a first at her age, but it was.

Definitely time to take some control of…

The SUV slid to a halt. Detra jumped out and opened Anne's door before she could. Seeing what was outside waiting for her, they might need the jaws of life to extract her from the vehicle. Splashed like a poster across the windshield, a Boeing 757—looking terribly long and sleek and painted in the blue-and-white livery of the United States of America executive aircraft—dominated her view.

But worse yet, the press corps was ranged behind a rope line and a phalanx of Secret Service agents, awaiting the Vice President's arrival and departure.

Except he wasn't here yet and every single one of those cameras were pointing at her vehicle.

Definitely time to return to not thinking about what was happening.

Then she heard a cry of police sirens and the cameras swung away…most of them.

# # #

Zack climbed out of the first SUV. The Secret Service had put him in the decoy vehicle and placed agents and the officer with the nuclear football in the limo behind. He never argued, Harvey said "go that way" and he went.

He headed for the rope line, Harvey had assured him that everyone there had been cleared and checked, so that he could approach without worry. That's when he spotted the lone SUV parked off to the right, yet on this side of the rope line.

Agent Detra Willand stood by an open door, looking into the vehicle with a puzzled expression on her face. He didn't know if he'd ever been happier to see a particular Secret Service agent in his six year association with them. If Detra was here, that meant—

Zack veered over to see what the problem was. As he peeked over Detra's shoulder he spotted Anne, rooted to the seat.

"Any problem, Agent Willand?"

She started. The first time he'd managed to surprise an agent. "Hello, Mr. Vice President. Sorry, sir. We appear to have hit someone's panic level."

"Mind if I try?"

Detra stepped out of the way, shifting into the protective circle that included Harvey and several others. He leaned in.

"Hi, Anne. Comfy? My, doesn't this feel familiar."

"That's a very big plane, Mr. Vice President," she didn't respond to his light tone.

He was so happy to see her here that he'd dance if that's what was needed and to hell with the press.

He gazed out the front windshield with her for a moment, "It is a big plane, isn't it? I believe that the President's is quite a bit bigger." He pushed for the double-entendre, but apparently it didn't catch.

"And that's a terrible number of reporters and cameras, sir."

"It is."

She didn't turn to him as she spoke, "I'm going home."

"I have two pieces of comfort for you to convince you otherwise."

"Which are?"

"Second, they're here to talk to me, not to you."

"What's first then?"

"I won't be the one flying that big beast. The largest fixed-wing plane I ever flew regularly is a glider, a sailplane. They're quite wonderful, you know. No engine, just you and the sound of wind. Really amazing."

She finally looked toward him, he could practically hear the snapping of the cords that had connected her to the aircraft and reporters. "You flew sailplanes?"

"Uh-huh."

"For the Air Force?"

"I was damned good at it too. Still have my license. Want to go up in one?"

She eyed him cautiously, "With you as the pilot?"

"Only room for two. Is that a problem?"

"Maybe."

Zack wondered what it would take to get Anne moving. He was sorely tempted to toss her over his shoulder and carry her to the plane. She awoke some primitive part of him that thought cavemen just might have had the right idea. He also thought that Anne would understand the joke…in the privacy of his own home. However, he'd been a politician long enough to know exactly how poorly that might be perceived by the press. He knew that while the Secret Service was circled close behind him, not far beyond them several dozen news service people would be assuming that he was busy necking with his girlfriend before he left on the flight.

He'd had worse ideas.

So he did.

After a muffled "mmfph" of protest, she gave as she always did: easily and completely. Anne Darlington played no games, held nothing in reserve. It was something that he both had no experience with and couldn't get enough of.

Then something shifted. He was no longer merely kissing a beautiful and willing woman. He couldn't identify the change, but was now kissing Melanie Anne Darlington. Whatever Alice had warned him of, Anne had made some decision and he was helpless before her.

Harvey cleared his throat behind him, once, then twice, then quite loudly.

Zack wanted to tell the man just how high a cliff he could go and jump off.

Someone bumped into him hard enough to jar apart his kiss with Anne.

Harvey mumbled a soft, "Sorry, Mr. Vice President."

Zack shifted back a few inches still under Anne's magic spell.

"You okay?" He whispered her.

"Not even a little," but she took his hand when he offered it. "North Pole would be simpler."

"But half the fun."

At the Press line he did manage to keep the questions directed to him, partly because Anne refused to speak. But there was no question about the photos on tonight's news, the Vice President holding hands with his girlfriend as they ascended the long steel stairway into Air Force Two.

# # #

When the big hatchway door closed behind them, Anne felt a surge of relief as visceral as diving into the swimming pond on hot day. In moments, she could hear the metal stairway rattling away and the engines began clawing to life.

"Oh my god. Please tell me that I never have to be doing that ever again in all my natural born days. Or any others."

"Depends. Are you planning to keep hanging out with me?"

She looked up at him. Zack was looking down at her… affectionately. The best kiss that any woman ever gave a man, and he was…still a man. She wanted to grab his shoulders and shake him, but the two Secret Service agents who had been last aboard the plane might tackle her to the carpet if she tried.

"Well? Are you?" This time she noted that though his voice was a tease, the eyes still hid the little boy.

"Get over it, sailplane boy. You're stuck with me. Even with that madness," she hooked a thumb out toward the scattering Press pool. Then she looked about for a distraction. "Can I get a tour? Our family jet would fit into this plane's overhead stowage bins."

There were four sections. First class had been replaced by a state-of-the-art communication system that completely humbled the First Lady's. You could run a war from here. Then she swallowed hard, that was *exactly* what you could do.

To the right, a narrow passageway slipped around the side of a blocked-off room. The door bore the Seal of the Vice President, the same as the President's except for a black outer ring and a white background on the center making it starker than the President's. That and the word "Vice," which Anne tapped lightly with a fingertip.

"You are like a drug, Anne," he understood her gesture. "A dangerous vice."

Okay, perhaps he'd been as affected by their latest kiss as she had. Maybe he was simply better at hiding it.

Zack swung open the stateroom door, and tossed his bag on one of the seats. Anne shrugged her shoulder and her knapsack plopped into the other executive brown-leather chair. His thick garment bag and her painfully thin one had somehow made it to the tiny closet ahead of them. There was a small desk between the two chairs, a tiny lavatory, and a three-seat couch that was long enough it might convert to a bed.

"How do you feel about joining the mile-high club?"

She took one look at the thickness of the walls on the stateroom—not very. "Dream on, Mr. Vice President."

He tried to pout, that was not going to work on her, before leading her out a second door and into the third section of the plane. Either side of the aisle had four business class seats facing small tables. Cornelia Day was already hard at work on whatever file came next. Other advisors and aides filled the additional seats.

Cornelia looked up at Anne and offered a genuine smile.

Anne returned it, "I don't have an answer for you yet, but I am working on it."

She acknowledged Anne's report with a sympathetic nod and returned to the paperwork laid out before her.

They both ignored Zack's puzzled, "What?"

The back of the plane had eight more rows of four seats each. A quick peek showed that most were filled with Secret Service agents. Detra and Harvey were in the front two seats. Beyond that, there was nothing more to see so they turned and headed back forward.

"What did you do to her?" Zack asked after they reentered his stateroom.

"To who?" Anne looked around and did her best to play stupid.

"Be glad I don't carry around a lie detector. Cornelia, that's who."

"What about her?"

Zack rolled his eyes.

"It's a girl thing, Mr. Vice President. I could tell you—"

"But you'd have to neuter me first. I get it. Forget that I asked."

"Anything you say, Mr. Vice President."

"Anything?"

Anne should have seen it coming, but Zack had been sneaky. Whether it was the Air Force Captain or the politician who'd set the trap, she wasn't sure. That didn't make it any less effective. He had locked both fore and aft stateroom doors without her noticing. He sat on the divan and scooped her against him as the plane's first motion unsettled her balance.

"You'd better take your time, Mr. Vice President, or we'll never make it to a mile-high," she whispered against his neck. "And if you aren't very quiet, I will kill you, treason or not."

Their clothes didn't even make it to the end of the taxiway. By the time they were powering down the runway, the plane wasn't the only one headed aloft.

# # #

Zack slipped from the bed so as not to wake Anne. Out the window fluffy clouds revealed a blue stretch of the Atlantic far below. They might have started while still on the ground, but making love to Anne Darlington had occupied him all the way to cruising altitude and then some.

As he was dressing, Zack watched her sleeping. Her hair spread over her face and down onto the blanket tucked up about her chin. He could see it many ways. Now blond, someday going to gray. Maybe one year short and the next longer again. He could imagine what he never had before, finding the same woman in his bed for all the days to come. To make love to a whole series of Anne Darlingtons separated from each other only by time.

Making love to Anne Darlington.

He'd had the thought before, but this day had been a repeated lesson in new perspectives. Anne had been defended by her sister-in-law Alice and had converted Cornelia to a staunch champion—something Zack knew was very difficult to achieve.

And then there'd been the President.

Zack had just been gathering up his papers when the President strode into his office and Zack knew that his chances of tracking down Anne before the flight had just dropped to zero. Peter Matthews hadn't moved like that when they'd campaigned together. He'd always walked with confidence, but now he moved with an inner surety. He strode forward and Zack knew it was his wife's doing. With a woman like Kim-Ly Geneviève Beauchamp Matthews behind him, a man couldn't help but be incredible.

He looked again at Anne asleep on his couch and knew the feeling exactly as he recalled the conversation.

"Hey, Zack."

"Mr. President."

But Peter Matthews didn't continue. He'd simply stood in Zack's office doorway and looked at him.

"Mr. President?"

He rubbed at his chin before speaking, another old habit. He'd seen the man redraft whole sections of speeches on the fly while making that simple gesture.

Didn't bode well.

"I'm not one to be telling you how to live your life, Zack…"

"But?" This could only be about one thing. "How does she gain such champions so easily?"

Peter smiled, "You'd have to ask my wife about that one. You're running in two years?"

No question on that topic either. "Someone has to fill your shoes when you're done with them, Mr. President."

"Thought so. Genny has her own ideas about you and Ms. Darlington; must say I agree with them—you two seem to fit well. But you also need to look to the future. You're never going to find a better woman to stand beside you."

"Christ, Peter," this conversation had just blown far past any honorifics. "We've been together less than two weeks. Give me a break."

"Nope," Peter just smiled at him. "Not when I've seen what I've seen. About time you began seeing it too. Safe trip, Zack. Bring us back a climate accord that has some real teeth in it and we'll find a way to get it passed." Then the President shook his hand and was gone.

Zack brushed back Queen Anne's long hair so that he could see her face as she slept on in Air Force Two's stateroom. They hadn't paused to convert Air Force Two's stateroom couch into a bed, his need for her too great after a day of dreading that she wouldn't travel with him at all and that she'd somehow slip away while he was in Italy.

He didn't know what President Peter Matthews had seen, but he agreed with him on one point, he'd never find a better woman to stand beside him. Now he had a new task, convincing her that he was worth standing beside.

He slipped out and closed the door behind him. He sat down opposite Cornelia in the conference area. She had slowly annexed the entire table until the other three occupants had moved elsewhere seeking a work surface. The paperwork was organized by country, environmental zone—air, water, soil, substrata—and market sector.

It took a moment to find his enthusiasm for the task; his mind was still with the woman asleep in the stateroom.

"When are you going to tell her?" Cornelia whispered without looking up.

"Tell her what?" Cornelia never whispered when she had something to say, though with four cabinet assistant secretaries sitting across the aisle, he appreciated it. He wasn't exactly comfortable discussing Anne Darlington even with those closest to him; he really didn't want the opinions of the Departments of Energy, Transportation, Interior, and Commerce as well.

"That you love her, you dolt."

Maybe he wasn't comfortable *at all* discussing Anne with those close to him. Not once had Cornelia Day ever addressed him by less than his proper title; not even when it had been the decidedly awkward Mr. Vice President-elect.

"What is it with you women?"

She didn't answer, but he could see her smile though she remained bent over her paperwork.

Zack decided to keep his mouth shut and focus on global climate change and ways to fix it. At least that he had a chance of understanding.

Chapter 7

If Anne had needed proof that she was in love, she found it on the ski slopes of Courmayeur. Because only a woman in love would be crazy enough to learn this ridiculous sport. Boots, bindings, skis, poles, thermal underwear, thermal waterproof pants, hats, goggles, inner gloves and outer mittens…she'd have needed less equipment to visit the International Space Station. She'd refused to give up her bulky parka and denied that ten degrees Celsius below freezing was merely nippy.

"Next time I lead an expedition, we're going to Tahiti. At least it has the right number of syllables."

"It what?" Zack slid to a neat stop and helped her once again rise from where she'd landed in a heap.

"Never mind."

"Though you in a bikini I think is an excellent idea."

"Not a chance, Mr. Vice President. I'm never taking off my parka, ever again. I'm going to be permanently chilled to the bone by this. And no, don't even think about making any jokes about helping me into a hot shower."

She could see by the smile showing below his sunglasses that was precisely what he'd been thinking.

After her fourth face plant into the snow, she'd was ready to jab Zack with a ski pole. She must not have been serious about it though or Harvey would have noticed and moved in closer to protect him. Secret Service agents swarmed the hill—some on skis, others on snowmobiles. And there was a large, treaded snow beast of a machine that rumbled suspiciously close by.

"Okay, it's beautiful. I'll admit that." They were high in the Italian Alps. The gondola ride from Courmayeur up the mountain had been spectacular, the town nestled in the heart of the valley below. The ski area was over the ridge and filled a bowl in the mountains. It felt as if the world was suddenly very far away. The air was biting, but it was also crystal clear in a way that Tennessee was on a cool autumn morning when the cut hay fields were still thick on the air and the first geese from the north passed by the farm's lake honking in dark Vs against the blue sky.

And it was her first fall in almost an hour. She'd graduated from the insultingly designated *bunny* slopes up to *facile*—even if "easy" was trying to kill her. Zack was proving to be a very tolerant teacher. Though she was sure that he'd be much happier zipping down those impossible cliff-like trails she'd caught glimpses of from the gondola, he hadn't given even the least hint of it.

A gondola ride into the Italian Alps with the best lover she'd ever imagined did make it difficult to complain. But she made the effort on his behalf.

"So this is what you do for fun?" They were quite close together, but because he was on the downhill side they were nearly eye to eye in height.

"Absolutely."

"Do you ride horses?"

"About as comfortably as you ski. I'm guessing you're good?"

"Remind me to show you my collection of blue ribbons. They cover a whole wall."

"Of your bedroom, Ms. Darlington? Is that an invitation?"

She couldn't let him have the victory that easily. "If you make a formal application for an entry visa, I'll take it under consideration." Then, before he could reply, she pushed off with her poles, aimed her ski tips downhill, and managed a turn without turning into a human snowball—a definite victory.

As she worked her way down the trail, down the *piste,* the mountains changed and shifted in every direction, except to the northwest. There, the Mont Blanc Massif soared above all the others, its many-fingered white peaks as distinctive as a fist raised against the sky.

Genny had said to look at the Massif and the country around it…she couldn't stop. The Great Smoky Mountains of Tennessee were soft, rolling hills worn with age. These mountains were tall, vibrant, filled with life. A tourist brochure that Anne had found on the villa's desk had pointed out that Mont Blanc was the third most heavily touristed natural wonder in the world, after the Grand Canyon and Niagara Falls. The tallest mountain in Europe, it dominated the skyline.

"That was amazing!"

"What was?"

Zack shoved against her shoulder and she tumbled into a snow bank…a snow bank at the foot of the lift. She turned and looked back up the slope, she'd skied the whole way down without another fall. She hooked a pole behind the Vice President's knees and yanked sharply forcing him to land beside her with a grunt.

"I *am* amazing!" She told him as she leaned in to kiss him.

"And don't you forget it." His admonishment made her hesitate.

She wasn't amazing. She was just Anne the-Vice-President's-girl-friend Darlington. Anne didn't turn aside from the kiss, but neither did it feel as incredible as it usually did.

She was rapidly becoming an adjunct to a spectacular man and that was a good thing, but it was far from being sufficient.

Zack pulled back to look at her, "Tell me what's wrong. How can I help?"

He couldn't. That was the real problem. No one could; it was something inside of her that was lacking. There was a desire, a focus, *an ambition* that others had but she'd never found. And that thought made her head hurt.

He'd risen to his knees—the Secret Service was moving in from the protective circle they'd formed to help him the rest of the way up. Anne grabbed the front of his ski jacket and yanked him back down into the snow, then kissed him hard.

Not thinking had worked well for her original plan. For now, she was going to stick with that.

Chapter 8

T he conference wiped out Zack's days and the dinner meetings took most of Zack's evenings. Other than that first afternoon on the slopes, his only time for Anne had been when she accompanied him to the dinners with other countries' representatives or when he curled up against her in utter exhaustion. Not exactly an opportune moment for pursuing his plan of discovering more about her.

Instead, she had listened while he raged against changes proposed and rejected—sometimes by his own "advisors" staunchly guarding their hidebound American thinking. She had made quiet suggestions that often worked to convince Japan or Iran to shift on one key point and Indonesia on another. And most of all she'd become an anchor that he couldn't imagine not finding in his bed every night. There were times when all he wanted to do was to lie quiet for even a minute with her curled up against him and her head on his shoulder.

She had known he needed a distraction and had told him of her own explorations while he'd been locked away discussing carbon credits and "clean" coal. Along with Detra, they had hiked some of the lower slopes of the massif.

"The wildlife here is incredible. We saw a mountain goat and a whole family of chamois—they're sort of half goat and half antelope. And we hiked up into whole fields of rhododendron that must be incredible when they're in bloom. There's a stark beauty here. I tracked down the local botanist and she said there are twenty-five hundred species and sub-species of flora, and that's just above the tree line. It's an incredibly rich environment. I was hoping to see a marmot, but they hibernate for up to ten months of the year, just as any sensible creature would in this frigid snowy place you have led me to."

The tease sounded and felt normal, but there was a sliver of reserve there since that kiss in the snowbank. Not that she gave less, but that she'd taken to deflecting even the subtlest of his inquiries about herself more than usual.

"Now's not the time," she'd whisper softly and sometimes they'd make love. Other times they would simply sleep still clinging to each other.

Well, for better or worse, the meetings were on hiatus for the day.

"A whole day together," he teased her in the shower. "Think that you can put up with me for that long?"

"It will be a burden, Mr. Vice President, but," she'd been scrubbing his back with a soapy washcloth, then she slid it down and forward between his legs, stealing his breath away. "Somehow I'll manage."

He turned on her and they both managed just fine.

A day off, he thought as he made a study of lathering her breasts, they could ski again. No, she worked down his chest and stomach until once more her hands were on the verge of killing him with pleasure, he wanted something different.

Ice skating? He pushed her back against the dark tile wall. No, still in the cold category.

Going into Milan or Turin for the day? His mind still worked as she wrapped her legs about his hips and her arms about his neck and he pressed her back against the shower's wall. Without warning the Secret Service ahead of time, that could cause problems.

If it was just him, what would he do? Anne clung to him as if she'd never let him go and Zack knew what the old saying "two bodies as one" truly felt like. He knew exactly what he'd do.

But first he had something to do here, and now he concentrated on it with all of his ability to give pleasure to another.

# # #

"Mr. Vice President, have I mentioned how stupid I think this is?"

"Several times," he replied from his sailplane seat close behind her. They both wore headsets so that she didn't even have to raise her voice to speak.

"Well, I'm saying it again. They dragged us up here, they can drag us right back down." At least she wasn't cold. She'd been freezing, until they closed the Plexiglas canopy and the tiny cockpit had warmed in the bright sun.

"See the red handle on the floor between your knees? Give it a good sharp yank."

Anne took one last look at the world she knew and wished it goodbye. The sky was Italian azure. The very tops of Mont Blanc's snowy peaks ranged at eye-level along the northern horizon. Far below, deep in the shadowed valley, lay the picture postcard town of Courmayeur.

Straight ahead flew a tiny tow plane attached to a long cable that once again bucked and jerked them about the sky. She heard that plane's engine grinding along ahead of them, and also felt the engine vibration transmitted to them down the cable. All about them the wind roared as if in a foul temper.

"We could be walking the Viale Monte Bianco. Green garlands over the street with wooden chicken ornaments dangling from them."

"Chickens? Really?"

"Really. And I discovered a charming little *trattoria*, just as Genny said I would, on the Via Roma. We could go in for a *caffe*. Because you're from Colorado, you can get a gelato even though it's the middle of winter. By evening, the every tree and bush will be lit with tiny white lights. And the crèche here is not a simple little tableau of statues; it has real people, donkeys, a manger, everything."

"Sounds wonderful. Let's go."

Anne waved her hand at the sky. "We can't because you have us ten thousand feet up in the air."

"Closer to fifteen thousand. Though Courmayeur is at four thousand, so we're close enough to ten thousand feet above the ground."

"Well get us down!" If she dared, she'd unbuckle, turn around, and throttle the man.

"So pull the red handle."

"But we don't have an engine."

"Soaring team captain my last two years at the Academy. We placed first nationally both years. Pull the release."

"Couldn't you have been a jet pilot instead like a normal Air Force captain?" Before she could think again, she gave the handle a yank.

The world changed as if they'd stumbled, or rather come off a stumble to find themselves at last walking gracefully. The cable dropped away in slow motion. The tow plane rocked its wings as if it was waving goodbye before it rolled on its side and plummeted down and away. With the cable detached, the flight of their sailplane smoothed out and she felt as if she was floating. The only sound now was the roar of the wind—which didn't seem nearly as malevolent as a moment ago—and the pounding of her heart.

Zack flew them along as smoothly as if they were on a rail, a rail across the sky.

Her feet were in the fiberglass nosecone, perhaps a quarter of an inch from the sky. There were four instruments: speed, compass, a miniature airplane floating along a horizon, and the last one ominously pointed at zero with the numbers one through five both above the zero and below it.

From the waist up she was surrounded by glass and sky. If she didn't turn enough to see the impossibly long and slender wings, she could be sitting alone in a chair ten thousand feet into the sky.

"Ready?"

"For this? No way. This is incredible."

"No, for this," the tone in his voice should have warned her as the nose tipped forward. That last traitorous instrument stopped pointing at zero and was soon pointing down at two, then three, then she was looking straight down at Courmayeur and the Dora Baltea River that flowed at the bottom of the Aosta Valley.

The moment before she could scream, the joystick between her knees—that must be attached to Zack's control—pulled right back into her lap. The sailplane's nose swung upward in a graceful effortless arc until she was looking straight up into the sky. They kept going, tipping on their back until she hung upside down and she now understood the reason for the four-point harness attaching her so solidly to her seat. And still she floated off it. Then with a lazy roll, the earth went from being over her head, to off the left side, and finally back to sensibly lying flat far below.

The rush of blood to her head eased back into her body, the floating freedom of it forced out a cry of delight that echoed in the tiny cabin. "That's better than sex, Zack."

"You're right, this was a bad idea. The first time you actually use my name, and it's to tell me that there's something better than sex with me."

She wanted to giggle as he swooped the plane downward in a lazy spiral. "It's the risk you take, Mr. Vice President."

"My ego is very bruised," he said lightly. As they spiraled, she could see the Secret Service's escort helicopter hovering to the south.

Harvey had thrown a fit, but Zack had convinced him that there was no mad saboteur lurking at the sailplane rental counter. Though they'd left an agent posted there to make sure that the clerk told no one about just who had taken one of their sailplanes aloft until they were safely returned.

Zack came out of the spiral into a wing-over-wing that rolled them all the way over sideways until they were right side up again with the same gentleness as them trading positions in bed.

"Your ego shouldn't be bruised. What's between us, that isn't sex."

"It isn't? Then what is it?"

"If I have to explain it, Mr. Vice President, it rather defeats the point."

# # #

Zack nosed the sailplane down again, just so that he could watch Anne's hair float up in the negative gravity. He kept pushing it over to do an outside loop, an entire loop in the sky, but with the cockpit turned to the outside instead of the inside of the circle. It was a tricky maneuver but he could still feel the proper control changes drilled deep into his muscle memory. The Schleicher ASK 21 sailplane was a solid performer and took them under effortlessly: nose aimed down, upside down at the bottom of the loop with the g-force dragging hard against them, finally nose straight up. Rather than going over the top and back to level flight to close the loop, he continued to drive the plane upward, bleeding off the speed until they hung suspended for a moment pointing straight up but going nowhere.

Then they began falling backward and he kicked the rudder pedal to twist them back into a nose-down dive. The thermal air currents coming up off the deep valley were sufficient that by the time he once again leveled out he had lost only five-hundred feet since releasing the tow; it was going to be a magnificent flight.

Flying *was* better than sex.

But it wasn't sex between them?

Then it was making love. And she was right, there was no need to explain.

Love is what passed between them. Love is what dug down warm and safe beneath the covers with them. It was the rich taste of that one special, private dinner they'd shared last night of Tagliatelle with Chestnut Flour in a Venison Sauce and a Controfiletto of Piedmontese Beef at the Pierre Alexis 1877 with the G-8 ministers. The massive brickwork arches, the winter flavors, and having Anne at his side all combined to make it one of the best meals of his life.

"This is slow food, Mr. Vice President," she had said. "That is why it is so good. It is never hurried along, and it is all locally sourced."

He couldn't agree more as he flew them high above the mountaintops of the Italian Alps. A sailplane was not about speed, it was about the joy of flight. A joy the woman seated before him provided at every moment in its purest form.

"I love you, Anne."

"I love you too, Mr. Vice President."

"And still she calls me by my title," he sliced a sharp bank toward the Massif, placing Mont Blanc itself dead center in the windscreen; a blinding snowfield glaring in the morning sunlight.

"Yes, sir."

"And what will you say when I ask you to marry me?"

"I will say no, Mr. Vice President."

The joystick slipped out of his fingers and he slammed against his harness as the sailplane stalled and twisted into a dive.

# # #

Anne barely had time to catch her breath before he recovered, but even she knew that the plane wasn't supposed to do what it had done.

"I'm sorry, Zack. Really I am. There could be no better man than you. But the answer will be no."

When he didn't respond, she wished she could turn to see him, but the harness made that impossible in little more than peripheral vision. Besides, she didn't know if she could stand to look at him.

How many sleepless hours had she spent on that very question?

She would be a good wife for a Vice President, perhaps even a good First Lady if he was elected.

…and she would become a wretched and bitter person. How much would he love her then?

Unable to tolerate the continuing silence, she finally removed the headset and simply let the roar of the wind fill her mind with white noise. She had taken all the joy out of the flight, but she hadn't expected the question, and so had answered it too bluntly. She could have been gentler about it but, now that it was out, she didn't know how to fix it.

No more exhilarating loops or flips. No stomach-dropping dives or stalls.

Zack simply flew them over some of the most beautiful landscape she'd ever seen and she did her best to not let him see her wipe at her eyes even though he sat directly behind her. The romance, the sensual play was gone as if it had never been.

He swirled them down the Aosta Valley, carved an effortlessly graceful turn, and brought them back toward Courmayeur.

They were lower now. They crested the brow of the ski area. The slopes were peppered with multitudes of skiers in colorful ski jackets against the white. Even though they were little more than dots from this elevation, she could now pick out the better skiers. They moved as smoothly as the Vice President flew his sailplane.

She tried not to think about the fact that she'd probably just lost any chance at "Zack" privileges and would soon be sent packing homeward on the next commercial flight out of Italy.

He swooped down over Courmayeur, caught in the throat of the narrow, steep-walled valley. Individual buildings were easy to see, despite their snow-covered roofs. The small villa where their nights had been so cozy. The tiny *trattoria* where she'd hoped to lead him tonight for penne with wild boar sauce and chocolate gelato. The large conference center that Zack would once again be immersed tomorrow, but now with her knife of refusal stabbed into his back.

"If I could take it back, I would," she whispered. But it did no good as her headset was clenched in her lap.

Instead, all she could do was look out at the near-vertical cliffs and—

# # #

"What's that?"

Zack barely heard. He'd been flying numb, which was a good way to kill them both. Even something as simple and forgiving as a sailplane called for constant attention to detail. He'd brought them too low and if they didn't find a good uplift, he'd never make it back to the airport.

Her answer would be *no?* That couldn't be right. Sure, it was far too soon to ask, but she already knew for certain that it was a no? Nothing had ever felt so right in his life, not his Air Force service or the two election nights where he'd been chosen as Vice President.

Anne was gesticulating off to the left. He glanced over and couldn't tell where she was pointing. He needed to figure out how to turn the plane in the narrow valley without catching a cliff wall, and get back out into the Aosta Valley.

He could see that she was yelling as she thumped her forefinger against the cockpit glass.

"Put on your damned headset if you have something to say, woman."

His growl of irritation must have been louder than he intended.

Anne scrabbled on her headset, still speaking as she did so.

"...d you see the explosion?" Again her fingertip pounding against the glass. "Look, there's another. Though the first one was way brighter."

He caught a small thermal at that moment and milked it for two-hundred feet of lift. As he did, he glanced left and caught a glimpse of what looked like a flash of sunlight off the snow cap atop the peak. Except the sun was at the wrong angle and the flash was instantly lost in a cloud of snow.

He found another couple hundred feet and saw a half-dozen dark figures standing back on a craggy limestone outcropping and throwing something out onto the snowfield. It was a motion he recognized, the same way you'd throw a...

Zack clicked on the radio that linked him to the Marine's Black Hawk helicopter following close behind, "Harvey." Anne went silent the moment Zack spoke. "Atop the ridge, ten o'clock from my position. Six, seven figures, tossing grenades. Do you have them?"

"Grenades?" Anne squeaked from the front seat.

"Hold, we're climbing for a better angle."

He started sliding in for a better view himself, when one of the distant figures made a different motion.

Zack slammed the joystick forward and right. There was a sharp slapping sound close behind him. A sound he knew too well. Though it had been a long time, it was impossible to forget.

"What was that?" Anne was twisting about looking for the source of the sound.

"We've been shot at, but all they hit was the plane," he tried to keep it light so that she wouldn't panic. No room for that up here.

"Are we going to crash? Are you hurt?"

"Interesting priorities there, I *feel* hurt. But *I'm* fine and so is the plane; I wonder if the insurance waiver will cover this. We have no engines, no fuel, and no hydraulics for them to damage. We're as safe as we can be without armor." And whatever bastard had just tried to hurt Anne was going to go down and go down hard. He keyed the radio again, "Harvey. People atop the ridge are armed and shooting. We took a couple hits, but we and our craft are five-by-five."

"Roger, Sidekick. Remain clear. Coordinating with Italian authorities."

"Sidekick?" Anne asked, impressively level-headed for someone who'd just been shot at, probably for the first time in her life.

"My whole family's Secret Service codenames were designated with to start with S. I'm Sidekick, naturally. Mom was Swimmer the one time she visited."

"And your dad is Sir."

Zack laughed. Even after ripping out his heart, she could still make him laugh. "Sidewinder, but yes, he is. He used to fly the F-14 Tomcats which packed the sidewinder missiles."

"That's…" Anne trailed off, twisting in her seat to look back toward the ridge. "Is that what I think it is?"

"I don't know, what do you…" But he didn't finish as he too turned and looked. His evasion had taken them farther up the valley and cost him some altitude, but they could still see the cliff face above the town.

What had changed was that a cornice of ice and rock had let go at the top of the mountain. Far more than would have happened naturally. It unfolded in slow motion, the first snow slip, an ice tumble, a rocky jut of the cliff. The first explosion that Anne had spotted must have been a more substantial device, followed up with grenades after the first one had broken the mountainside loose, but hadn't quite knocked it off. It certainly had now, the entire cliff face was in motion.

The slide began losing form and mutated into a seething curtain of boiling rock and ice.

"They started an avalanche. We have to warn the town," Anne cried out.

"No time." And there wasn't.

They could only watch in horror as it picked up speed. Within seconds, the jumble of ice and rock reached the tree line.

Twenty-foot conifers were swept up like matchsticks. Farther down the slope, sixty-foot larch and spruce fell just as easily. The shattered trees only made it easier to see how broad and fast-moving the avalanche was.

Small chalets which perched on the lower slopes disappeared. Below them lay the town.

The valley was so narrow at this point, practically choking Courmayeur into two pieces, that there was little for the avalanche to hit. But what was there was hit and hit hard.

The river and the road were buried. And the biggest building in the whole town, the conference center—where they were supposed to be meeting today but had taken a day off to allow tempers to cool—disappeared beneath a blizzard of snow and a crushing load of ice, rock, and trees.

Chapter 9

There are people down there," Anne looked down at the wreckage. This couldn't be real. Moments before there had been an idyllic stretch of a beautiful mountain town climbing through a narrow pass up into the main village. Now the entire width of the pass was nothing but chaos.

"Harvey," was Zack's answer. "Patch me through to Aviano Air Force Base, encrypted."

When Harvey responded, she could hear gunfire in the background over her headphones. Zack turned the plane and glided back over the wreckage. Even as she looked down, she saw someone crawl out from under the snow and flop to the ground. "Survivors, Zack."

"I know," his voice was a growl.

That more than anything helped Anne return to the moment. She had to work the last sixty seconds backwards to make any sense of it.

Conference center that was hosting the International Climate Change and Control Conference destroyed.

Avalanche.

Explosives.

Men throwing explosives.

That first massive flash she'd seen.

The first big explosion hadn't unleashed the avalanche as someone had hoped. But they'd thrown enough grenades afterward to finally break it loose.

Terrorists. Some terror group who didn't like the I4C conference. Never in her life had Tennessee felt so far away as this instant. The farm was safe, familiar…this was horrific.

"This is Aviano tower, go ahead," she heard over the headset.

"I need to speak with your commanding officer."

"And who is placing this request?"

"This is Captain Zachary Thomas, USAF (retired) and the Vice President of the United States. Get a move on!"

It took only seconds and Zack was describing the situation to a colonel. Then he began issuing rapid-fire orders, "I need you to scramble every helo pararescue team you've got on-base and tell them to bring their dogs. We need Search and Rescue as well as medical elements. The flights are not to enter the valley directly, we don't want to trigger a secondary avalanche. Have them land in the town or in fields to the far side. And not to pull rank that I don't have, Colonel, but move it."

It would have taken a stronger man than the colonel or a stronger woman than herself to argue when Vice President Zachary Thomas used that tone.

"Pararescue?" She didn't know the term.

"You might have heard of them as PJs, parajumpers. The Air Force PJs are the toughest warriors out there. Ever wonder who Delta or SEALs reach when *they* dial 911 from the center of a battlefield? It's the PJs. I flew with them as pilot for most of my career."

"I thought you only flew…sailplanes," she suddenly felt deeply foolish. She should have known that someone like Zack had done so much more than fly a sailplane and fix someone else's jet. That's what she'd guessed, because he was so competent about everything he did. The train engineer turned jet engineer, but she'd been so wrong. He flew into the center of battles to rescue people.

"Fixed wing, this is the biggest plane I've flown. Put me in a Sikorsky Black Hawk and that would feel like home far more than One Observatory Circle. How did you not know that about me?"

He circled them down lower.

"I didn't want to use the Internet to get to know you. It seemed like an unfair advantage going into the relationship. I remember 'military service' from your campaign, but that's all."

His voice was a low growl that she could barely hear over the wind's roar as they circled downward, "Yet another reason to appreciate the goddamn woman who won't have me."

Anne decided that it was best to pretend she hadn't heard or else she'd start crying. Maybe even beg to take back her own words, though she knew they were the right ones.

"There," with a hard bank they swooped down toward the beginner's ski slope that had caused her so much trouble just a few days ago.

"Sir, what are you doing?" Harvey sounded livid. "Return to Corrado Gex Airport immediately. That's an order, sir." Gunfire still echoed in Anne's headset. She finally spotted the helicopter still high above the valley. It was in a hard bank, a line of tracer fire arced from its side across the blue sky like a golden laser beam. Even as she watched, it twisted hard in the other direction, but the line of gunfire merely changed angle to remain on target.

"Out of range," the Vice President spoke in that tone again. "We're landing here, Harvey. You just make sure none of those bastards gets away. Sidekick out."

For the next sixty seconds Anne alternated between holding her breath and fighting a scream that kept trying to emerge from her chest. She didn't know if it was the near misses with the tops of towering spruce, the low cables of the chair lift, or the occasional skier rushing right in front of them as they raced toward the calamity. Perhaps it was her own rage at what had just been done to the innocent people of this town.

"Who, Zack? Who would do this?"

"Insane environmentalists. Even more insane jihadists. Sick psychopaths. Doesn't matter. Not our concern right now."

"Right," she looked at the fast approaching snow field. "Our concern is surviving the landing."

"Oh ye of little faith. *Our* concern is helping those people." Even as he spoke, he landed on the snow field. They skidded along for a heart-stopping few hundred feet—missed two skiers by inches, eased to a stop, and then in an incredible anticlimax, tipped gently to the side until one wingtip rested delicately on the snow. Within seconds, they were both out of the aircraft and racing toward the disaster.

# # #

For Zack, the next hours passed in a blur.

Zack and Anne had joined the other villagers converging on the area of the slide. The few who had managed to rescue themselves were tended to or carried off. Then began the arduous task of calling out and digging.

Anne had a natural flair for organizing panicked people into useful work parties and they soon had clear markers up defining areas which had been searched. The ski patrol came down off the mountain and offered their skills and manpower, but Anne remained in charge of whole sections of the effort.

Zack hadn't done this level of brute force labor since the Air Force and was soon solely focused on the task in front of him. Call, listen, step. Call, listen, step. Dig down into rock, ice, or rubble if there was even a hint of a sound.

Eventually Harvey had landed and tried to extract him, and almost earned a fist in the face for his troubles. Zack's anger needed a direction. His anger at the senseless violence and death that six years in war zones had not inured him to.

His anger at the attackers. And underneath, his pain at Anne's unexplained refusal.

Ultimately Harvey and the other Secret Service agents had collected around him and they'd all worked together as a team. The Marines had the only helicopter in the area, which was rapidly converted from security to medevac.

Then pararescue jumpers and a half dozen combat-search-and-rescue dogs had parachuted down out of the sky like angels from heaven. The search began moving much faster with the CSAR dogs' keen senses and the PJs' incredibly advanced skills. The fatalities were light, but the casualties were soon overwhelming hospitals as far away as Milan. Helicopters, both American and Italian, were soon dotting every open field, rushing out the injured, rushing in with aid.

Night fell, lights came on, and the work continued. The work turned deeply grim when they reached the conference center. The representatives who had decided to work through the day had been caught. They uncovered people he knew, had talked to, fought with, and respected. They were now battered, freezing to death, or worse. The fatality count which had remained in the teens for some hours rose sharply and passed fifty before the night was through with no signs of abating soon.

It was late afternoon of the next day before he was dragged away, no longer able to do much more than stumble about. The American delegation had been missing four. Two they'd found in a shattered corridor, the other two were found hours later around four a.m.—very much alive and happily sharing body warmth beneath the conference table that had saved their lives.

Ready to drop in his tracks, Zack knew that he was becoming more of a hindrance to the operation than an asset. Time to pull back, regroup. Most of the other delegates had returned home. There would be another conference at another time. Many had sought him out among the wreckage to shake his hand and promise that they too would return to finish what had been begun. Others had worked beside him for a time until one by one it became clear that political delegates were not up to professional rescue standards and were escorted away by their security teams.

Harvey had let him fight on until he was one of the last, but between the increased size of his Protection Detail—under threat of renewed terrorist activity—and the news coverage that had discovered him laboring in the midst of the disaster, he was causing more problems than he was solving.

The retreat didn't stop at the hotel room. He was soon swept aboard the same Marine Two helicopter that had wiped out the terrorist cell—with their still-unknown affiliation. They had fought to the last man and died just that way. No one had stepped forward yet to claim the deed.

Marine Two whistled due to the many holes that the terrorists' bullets had punched, but it reached Milan safely. Air Force Two was in the air before his brain clicked into place and he missed Anne—an oversight he might never forgive himself.

"Where is she?"

Harvey didn't answer, he was passed out in his seat. Of the few still awake, no one knew.

Zack grabbed Harvey's shoulder, finally had to shake him hard to rouse him. Harvey came to with a fist headed for Zack's jaw. Despite starting from a dead sleep, it connected hard enough to send Zack tumbling backward to land in the laps of the two agents across the aisle. One grunted in his sleep, one didn't even do that.

"Oh my god. I'm so sorry, Mr. Vice President," Harvey struggled up out of his seat. "Are you okay, sir?"

With Harvey's help, Zack clambered out of the two sleeping agents' laps. He rubbed at his jaw. It wasn't broken. He checked his aching teeth with his tongue and detected no chips. But oh brother, it was going to hurt for a while.

"Is that how you wake up? When you find a wife, she's in trouble, Harvey."

"Uh. Are you sure you're all right, Mr. Vice President?"

Zack patted the agent's shoulder, reminding himself to never do that again with a sleeping Secret Service agent. "Nothing that time won't heal, Harvey. Sorry to wake you," he worked his jaw again and a jolt of pain was his reward, "more sorry than I'd expected. Where's Anne?"

Harvey blinked at him stupidly for a moment.

"We need to turn back and get her. She's—" Zack started to turn for the cockpit.

"She's already gone, Mr. Vice President." Harvey rested a restraining hand on Zack's elbow. "Sorry, I assumed you knew. She flew out this morning. Commercial flight. Destination Tennessee."

Zack eyed Harvey and was just tired enough to consider returning the favor of fist to jaw.

"Gave me a note," he found it and handed it over.

Zack read the single line. "You were wonderful." *Were!* Past tense.

Harvey must have spotted the rage that swept over Zack.

He held up both hands as if in surrender, perhaps in retreat. "Through Agent Detra Willand. I never saw Ms. Darlington, Mr. Vice President, or I would have made sure that you saw her. Detra said she worked like a demon until the PJs got a command-and-control team in place. Only then she collapsed. After the medic cleared her, she caught a ride to the Milan airport with the British minister."

"Where's Detra?"

"Escorting Ms. Darlington home."

Zack wished there was a chair handy for him to collapse into, but they were all occupied by sleeping agents. Some of their clothes were still wet, many torn, only two still had ties. They had scrapes and bruises, one had his arm in a sling. He probably didn't look any better; they'd battered themselves against the disaster right alongside him.

"Harvey, when these guys wake up, tell them that I'm giving each of them a thousand dollars out of my own pocket to spend on their families this Christmas. Christ knows they deserve something better than that, but it's a good start."

Harvey hesitated.

"You too. I know you have no one special for Christmas, though you damn well should."

"I'm not the only one who should, sir."

Zack grimaced. He'd barely had time to absorb the idea that he'd found the only woman for him, before Anne had slapped that down hard. "Just don't spend it all at the horse races," he dodged Harvey's sympathy.

"Yes, sir," and then he smiled. "Awfully sorry about the chin, Mr. Vice President."

Zack offered his best nonchalant shrug and ignored the pain in his jaw; Harvey had really caught him. He went back to the 757's VIP stateroom. He almost crashed face-down onto the couch, but he was just exhausted enough that he could still see Anne lying there, curled up asleep after they'd had sex.

No, damn it! They'd made love. He knew the damned difference.

Then he dropped into his chair.

He just didn't know what to do about it.

Chapter 10

*A*nne *arrived at the* Darlington Estates Farm in far worse shape than she'd left it, which was really saying something. She'd left in a fit of pique, wishing there was some way, any way out of her own life.

An idyllic affair with a powerful and wonderful man.

An Italian getaway.

And she'd been the one to find the remains of the Thai Minister of the Environment, whom she'd recognized by the Old World cufflinks that he'd worn to one of the dinners…there'd been little else to identify him by, though she was doing her best to block out that particular memory.

He'd been the first of many. Though there had been the miracle moments as well. She'd seen fewer and fewer of either as the relief effort took some shape and her role shifted away from the front line itself. Her ability to organize dinner and entertainment for five hundred guests had translated surprisingly well. "Winery Tour" in her mind became the search through the bar and night club that had also been demolished by the avalanche.

The "Main Meal" was naturally the conference center hall and meeting rooms. The "Kitchen Tour," an ever-popular viewing before a Darlington dinner, was all of the staff and help areas. The "Crops Tour" started working the open field and roadways. "The Stables" were all of the little chalets.

Thankfully, it had been mid-morning and there was a day's hiatus of the meetings, so most of the people had been out of the building. Had the attack been planned as a demonstration with minimal casualties? Or had they not known about the hiatus and intended to kill both government officials and townspeople alike? None of the answers reached her. Detra also claimed no further knowledge.

Three Caucasian, three Arabic. No IDs. Mercenaries for some industrial super-conglomerate? A personal vendetta against some single member at the conference?

The Vice President's decision to attend had indeed escalated the rank of politician that every country had sent and thus increased the value of the target.

For the hundredth time she wished she'd never left home. Had merely watched the disaster as some obscure news piece on television. She'd never confronted death in any form more violent than a clean hospital bed or under hospice's gentle care.

Zack had been magnificent. She'd kept receiving reports about some group who wouldn't identify themselves, but were proving very effective. They covered twice the ground of anyone other than the PJs. She'd finally gone to see who they were for herself and had spotted Zack and his phalanx of Secret Service agents lifting sections of a collapsed roof. Mother, child, dog, and a form wrapped in a sheet had emerged. They were handed off to the medical teams and Zack had moved on to the next structure.

She had retreated back to her temporary headquarters in a single-car garage that had been untouched by the devastation. There she had continued until she could barely see the three-man military team that came to take over from her.

Anne had thought about going to Zack, but what more was there to say? He hadn't seriously proposed, but she'd ended the relationship just as thoroughly as if he had when she turned him down.

When the British Minister of the Department of Energy and Climate Change had offered her a lift to wherever she wanted to go, she took it. Sitting in the car morphed into gathering her belongings at the untouched hotel where she couldn't bear to imagine Zack finding her. The first step toward home had become a second, then a third. By the time she'd reached Milan, she was on a conveyor belt back to the farm; every choice turned toward Tennessee right down to two open seats on a one-stop flight to Charlotte, North Carolina leaving in an hour.

Her mother had taken one look at Detra and herself and sent them both off to bed without questions.

Anne didn't remember undressing, but must have because she'd woken to find her clothes in a heap on the carpet.

Now she sat on her bed, showered and dressed in fresh clothes, but with no energy to do more despite a dozen hours of near catatonic sleep. The broad queen size four-poster bed that had rarely seen a man let alone a husband. The flowered curtains and matching bedspread: ivy twined improbably with buttercups and field daisies. Oaken bookshelves with dressage trophies from high school and steeplechase from college. She barely recognized it as her own room after the last two weeks.

With the changes that she had gone through, that her heart had gone through, it was impossible that she was still the same person. She held up a hand and twisted it back and forth. It was definitely hers and it was attached solidly enough to her arm, so she must be herself. Even if she didn't feel it.

A soft knock and her mother slipped into the room. She looked completely the Tennessee matriarch. Leather, knee-high riding boots. Snug black slacks. A white, pleated-front blouse exquisitely tailored to advertise both figure and wealth without ostentation. Her gold-blond hair a perfect coif. Minimal makeup on her clear skin. Mary Annette Darlington fit her looks well, thoughtful and kind with a spine of steel when needed. Except now she looked very worried.

"Can you talk about it yet, dear?"

Anne could only shake her head no.

Her mother came in, closed the door quietly, and then simply gathered Anne against her bosom. She smelled of talcum powder and ever so slightly of horse. She'd already had her morning ride. It was the smell of home.

"Agent Willand caught me up over breakfast. Italy sounds awful."

"Parts of it."

"You're not in the news."

Anne flinched.

"And no, I'm not telling anyone about how wonderful you were. There's marketing, and there's my baby girl. Guess which one wins."

It was an old routine going back as far as she could remember. "Baby girl always wins," they said together, but Anne was unable to join in the laugh.

"They'll figure it out at some point, but Zachary Thomas has made such a big splash I just may have to vote for him myself when the time comes." Which was quite a concession because her mother had always voted straight line for the other party. "Is he really as wonderful as he appears to be?"

"He's better."

Her mother let her go and rose from the bed, then sat in another chair and scooted it up until their knees were practically touching. In front of them, a grand arched window looked out across the fallow winter fields, the big horse barn of natural wood with a green roof. Beyond it ranged the misty Smokies of the Cherokee National Forest, as familiar as the feel of her own hands and as foreign now as remote wilderness.

"Now, child. I know that face. That's a face I've watched since the day you were born to light up the world. But it's not being very lit at the moment."

"Vice President Zachary Thomas proposed." Anne hadn't meant it to slip out like that, hadn't meant to tell that to anyone, anywhere, ever.

"Might quick by my reckoning, but he's a wise man. Knows when he's met the best woman he ever will. Other than myself of course, but I'm taken after all and old enough to be his mother no matter how hard I do try to not look it."

She wanted to snap at her mother. There was nothing special about Anne Darlington. But Anne had made the mistake of saying that before and her number one fan, her mother, had stepped up to the plate. From there she'd line-driven the initial pitch right back down her throat, in front of Jeffrey L. Walters and his family. Jeffrey, the only even marginally decent candidate before Zachary, wisely had run for the hills.

Her mother couldn't seem to see the truth. There was nothing special about her. Pretty, wealthy, polite, and from a socially powerful family. None of that sounded like it had anything to do with her.

"What did you tell him?" Her mother asked it like a foregone conclusion.

# # #

"She turned you down?"

Zack could only stare into his whiskey and nod. He was slouched on the couch in the Oval Office.

He'd come straight from the plane, a flight for which only he and the pilot had been awake. The President had taken one look at him, pointed toward a couch, and poured three fingers of whiskey. He was down by two with one finger to go. The problem was that, if it was football and not whiskey, the fourth down was over before he'd even had a chance to call the play.

"Said it almost without my asking. 'If you ask me, I will say no, Mr. Vice President.' She even calls me that during sex—I'm mean when we're making lo—" He rubbed the glass against his forehead, but the President had poured it neat rather than over ice so it did nothing to cool his brow. "Sorry, too much information."

Peter shrugged that it was okay. "I'm so sorry, Zack. I really thought she was the one for you."

"Thank you, Mr. President. I was starting to think that myself."

The last finger of whiskey had gone somewhere and the President refilled his glass. Reset the ball, three fingers to go. Maybe by then he'd be down.

"You earned a lot of good will in Italy. The rescues. Calling in your old pararescue unit. It will stand you in good stead next year."

"Let's just make sure the next conference is somewhere flat, like Nebraska."

"Deal. I think you can make any plan you want after your performance over there, both before and after the attack. You saved the lives of dozens of countries' top politicians. I know it was awful, but it was still well executed."

"That's not why I did it," Zack stared down into the whiskey. Anne would know why, knew why. There had been no question as they landed the sailplane and sprinted to help, helping was just what people did. Or should do. So few did, but Anne, with no military training, had raced to help.

"I know that's not what motivated you," the President said patiently. "Of course I know that. But I'm trying to find you some light from the situation, buddy."

"And why is he in need of light?" Genny Matthews came striding in, looking like her normal million dollars in a soft green dress that complemented the room's Christmas ornaments. "*Merde!* Zachary you look awful."

"Perfect. Goes exactly with how I feel."

"Anne turned him down." Zack was glad that the President was there to explain, he didn't think he could say it again without his heart dying.

"You ask her already?" Genny spun on him. So much for someone else taking the front-line defense.

"No! Yes. Not really. She said, 'I love you, Mr. Vice President.' I asked what she was going to call me when I asked her to marry me and she said, 'I will say no, Mr. Vice President.' I don't exactly call that encouraging."

Then the irate First Lady turned on her husband and Zack once again hoped for relief. "And what do you say to him when he tell you that his heart is broken."

"He said no such thing," Peter Matthews held up his hands in self defense. "I told him I was sorry. What else was I supposed to do?"

The First Lady made a noise deep in her throat like a Black Hawk engine that was grinding to life but had no fuel. Zack wondered if the President would be sleeping on the couch tonight. Then he wished he hadn't thought that because it reminded him of Anne sleeping on the couch on Air Force Two and that led him back to...

Whiskey.

His second glass was only a finger down.

Two to go.

Would six fingers of whiskey get him a new down? Ten earn him a first down plus yardage? No. It would get him a blinding headache and solve nothing. Regretfully he set aside the remaining two fingers.

"What are you going to do about it?"

"About what?" He looked up at the First Lady who was still storming back and forth in front of his couch. "I think I lost the thread of the conversation."

"About Anne?"

Zack shrugged, "She said no."

Genny Matthews stared at him in disbelief for a long moment, then smacked her palm against her forehead.

Chapter 11

*T*his is Anne," she almost hadn't answered her cell phone. She didn't trust unlisted numbers. She hadn't even known there was cell reception out here at Beau Ridge.

"Hold please." And some thin thread of Southern politeness had her agreeing and in moments she was listening to Christmas carol hold music. She was sitting on top of her favorite horse, looking at the most beautiful vista in the entire Smokies: the forests behind her, the rolling foothills and the farm below, and in the distance the sun glinting off Boone Lake.

Christmas was only days away and she knew she was going to be a crashing bore on the family. She was past being able to help herself and her mother had merely patted her hand and promised, as she always did, that things just had a way of naturally turning out for the best. Ma was even right on occasion, but not this one.

To shake off her depression, for her family's sake if not her own, Anne had saddled up Mephista. Her blood bay mare was part sweetheart and part she-devil. She was also a true dark red with a charcoal black mane and tail that reached down to her hocks which only made her more dramatic—and didn't the mare just know it.

Anne had ridden across the farm fields and up into the Cherokee National Forest before Detra awoke. The Secret Service had been on the verge of recalling Detra, and Anne had worried about the loss of the agent's cheery take on the world—it was all that had kept her sane these last few days. Then the news of Anne's own participation in the Italian disaster recovery had broken.

For days Anne had been obsessed with the ongoing news coverage of the event. Perhaps by the intense media focus on Zack as well, but she wasn't going to admit that to her mother or herself.

Then yesterday her own face had appeared on the screen.
VP's Girlfriend Saves The Day!
Anne Is Disaster's Darling!
Where is Anne D.?

Some PJ, answering questions before his unit pulled out at the close of the search-and-rescue effort, had offhandedly referred to the exceptional initial coordination by "a Ms. Darlington" that could be credited with directly saving dozens of lives if not more. He then quietly disappeared back behind his anonymous Special Operations smoke screen and received no more attention than a horse gave a kitten—one or two sniffs from the media and then a careful step around.

The Tennessee farm, on the other hand, had been stormed by reporters and the Secret Service had left her protection in place, even added a few more agents. She only felt a little guilty for escaping and leaving it for Detra and her mother to handle today.

Out here she was alone. Beau Ridge was where she'd always come as a girl, riding Jolie before she'd learned the skills to ride Mephista. Jolie was now a dozen seasons gone and Mephista was showing signs of gray on her muzzle, though she showed no hints of easing down some. More than the house, out here was Anne's home. The quiet place where there was no one but her and her horse. She couldn't even see the house from here, though most of the farm was visible. Tall trees and rolling hills masked the buildings.

The air was chill enough that she could see her breath, but there'd been no frost on the ground. Here was her place and she was alone at last.

Except for the stupid Christmas carols.

It was all Darlington land for miles around, one of the grand old southern plantations saved by generations of hard labor. Beyond the eastern side of the property the Smoky Mountains were wrapped in the cool fog that gave them their name. She'd always liked the ride up to Beau Ridge through the cove hardwood forest. It was the most diverse biome anywhere in the country; yellow birch, basswood, sugar maple, and magnolia dominated this section of it. The trail circled low around the back of the ridge, with the sweeping vista as a surprise exit from the woods.

The Christmas carol on the phone changed to one she really didn't want to hear. It had been sung by the Congressional Hearings acapella group and they'd done a much better job. She should get Zack to pass a law against Muzak; not that she still had any link to him.

Anne was on the verge of hanging up when the operator finally returned to say, "I'll connect you now."

A sudden chill shook her enough for Mephista to look up from the grass she'd been cropping. If this was Zack, she'd—

"*Bon chance*, Anne. We have reached you. That is so very good. I'm sorry, I could not make the New Zealand Ambassador hang up sooner without being rude."

"Uh. Hello Ms. Matthews."

"None of that, Anne. It is Genny. You know this. Tell me about the Mont Blanc Massif."

"I don't want to—" But Genny hadn't asked about Courmayeur, or the disaster, or the disaster that she'd made of things with Zack.

She should have said goodbye to him, but hadn't been able to face him to do so. It was her greatest regret, because it had been cruel and cowardly.

"The Massif?"

"*Oui!* Did you know that just twenty percent of World Heritage sites are natural? The rest we call cultural, man-made. We have so very many applications for more to be named and protected, but I do not understand them well. So, when I work with the UN, I can not do the natural ones justice as they need. Tell me of the Massif, the flora and fauna, whatever you know. I visited Chamonix on the other side of the Mont Blanc Massif, but all I see were skiers and *le charmant village.*"

"First, if you are in Italy, you must call it the Massiccio del Monte Bianco or they will not speak to you." Anne found herself sliding easily into the topic. Genny was a very willing audience and they were soon discussing details Anne was only peripherally aware of having learned on her days while Zack was in meetings, as she and Detra had hiked or chatted with the Italians of Courmayeur. Once she'd learned to name it properly, the locals had been only too happy to talk about their region of the Alps.

Anne dismounted and tied Mephista's reins to a handy tulip tree. Jolie had always grazed placidly wherever you left her, Mephista would wander off just for spite.

"Oh, that is all so very helpful. It will be perfect when you come to Washington."

"When I—"

"You will teach me and I will teach you. I never knew so much about how the wilderness is affected by the cultural pressures. Well, I know this, but I am not so good as you at putting it into words. And working with the UN ambassadors we have need to put it into words scientifically, but not in a way they won't understand. You have the knowledge, the family name, and—I am ashamed to say it so bluntly—the class that is necessary to work with them."

"But—"

Genny's smooth voice and soothing accent were backing Anne into a corner until it felt as if an avalanche of words was landing upon her.

An avalanche.

One of those in a lifetime was enough.

"I'm sorry, Genny," Anne broke in. "But I'm not coming back to Washington, DC. Nor to the UN in New York."

"Oh but of course you are," Genny didn't sound the least bit unsure. What would it be like to be a woman without doubts? Anne couldn't even imagine.

She leaned her forehead against Mephista's neck. The horse's fur was coarse and familiar. The horse turned enough to snort at her hair, the mare's breath a warm wind across the back of Anne's neck.

"I..." She thought back over their talk, then checked her watch. Most of an hour had gone by and it had happened in an eye blink. "I loved talking to you about this project. It's fulfilling to use what I studied in school and on the farm to good end. Perhaps I could work with you on something again..." Anne steeled her resolve, "...remotely. Like this. From here. Not in—" She clamped down on her tongue before she sounded completely infantile.

Genny's laugh was utterly delighted. "I told you that you and I would become such good friends. I can not wait to see you again soon."

"Didn't you hear me?" Didn't anyone hear her? Her mother had told her everything would be fine. Genny was convinced that she would... "I'm not returning to DC. Not while," she swallowed hard but couldn't manage his name, "he's there."

"But Zachary is not here."

"Then where is he?" And Anne cursed herself for falling into the trap of wanting to know.

"Why he is there," Genny said with absolute confidence. "You must look around, my good friend Anne. There is a whole world waiting for you."

"What do you mean he's *here?*"

Then she raised her head and peeked over Mephista's dark withers. "Oh shit!" Then she clamped a hand over her mouth to block any other foul language.

Somewhere in a distant corner of her mind, Genny's laugh was a merry ringing of bells.

In the foreground, not even a hundred yards away, Zack Thomas was riding up the trail with Harvey and two other agents in tow. Zack rode as naturally as he did everything else. Harvey managed; the other two would be lost at the first low tree branch.

If she were mounted, she'd run. No one could catch her in these hills if she rode Mephista.

Except maybe Zack, who rode his saddle far more magnificently than she skied, even though he did hold the English bridle western style. No hat or gloves, he wore a sheepskin jacket that he hadn't bothered to button over his sweater. The man was part polar bear. He should go to the North Pole with Santa and the elves and leave her alone. But he was here.

He was *here!*

No one knew about this place, not her mother, not anyone. Oh.

They'd traced her phone while she spoke to the First Lady about the Mont Blanc Massif and UNESCO World Heritage, the first intriguing idea for Anne's future that she'd ever come across.

She ducked her head back down behind Mephista's neck and spoke into the phone.

"Friend or not, I'll get you for setting me up like this, Genny."

"Good. I am looking forward to it, because you must come to Washington to do this to me. *Au revoir!*" And the phone went dead.

She peeked back over Mephista's neck. Zack was still there, looking even better than he had a moment before.

# # #

Zack knew he shouldn't be grinning; he was facing the woman who had told him no. But after he dismounted and walked up to the other side of the beautiful red mare and looked at Anne across the horse's withers, he couldn't help himself.

"God, but it's good to see you, Anne."

She ducked her face out of sight again so that all he could see was the top of her head as her face rested against the bay's black mane.

He moved in so that he'd be right there when she popped back up again, but Anne's horse had other ideas. He saw the horse try to swing her hindquarters into position for a kick, but he knew the motion and shifted toward her head. The mare was smart enough to anticipate, perhaps even have planned on that, as she swung her head to nip at him. Only good reflexes saved him from the sharp click of her teeth inches from his arm. Then she gave a snorting horse laugh. Yes, she'd known exactly what she was doing.

"I don't think your horse likes me very much."

Anne looked over the withers again, only her eyes and the top of her head showing. "Mephista is a very smart horse."

Mephista. Devil horse. Of course Anne Darlington would ride such an animal. "Is there any chance of us speaking without an ornery horse between us?"

"No!" She said it sharply enough that the horse turned a worried look in Anne's direction. "And she's not ornery, she's... lost." The last word was a bare whisper.

Zack tied his own horse's reins to the same tree as Anne's, then circled around the tree until he was on the same side of the red mare as Anne. The agents all dismounted with a look of relief and moved off to set up a perimeter, which wasn't necessary, and to give him and Anne a little space, which he didn't know what to do with.

He rested his hands on her shoulders and slowly turned her to face him. He didn't expect what he saw when he did; he'd never seen Anne cry before and it undid him. At a loss for what else to do, he pulled her into his arms and she didn't fight him. She lay her head against his shoulder for a long while, not sobbing but merely sniffling from time to time.

When he stroked her hair she moved back and then another step until she bumped into her horse. She wiped at her eyes with gloved fingers, then looked up at him. It was clear that she wasn't going to speak first and this was up to him. He wished Genny was here—she'd rounded on both him and her husband about what idiots they were. Maybe that was the place to start.

"Genny says that I'm an idiot."

Anne didn't leap to his defense as some part of him had hoped, instead she eyed him as speculatively as her horse had.

"She did a good job of making her point."

Anne nodded, "She does that. Why are you an idiot?"

Okay. Definitely not leaping to his defense. "It's not completely clear. She had many, many points. I think the main one is that I'm a crappy listener."

Anne squinted at him in thought. By the tip of her head he'd say that she didn't agree, but wasn't sure enough to argue the point either.

"You came to Washington looking for what *you* wanted to do."

"I did," her surprise told him that that fact had been lost for her as well.

"You swept me off my feet from the first moment I saw you, Anne, and I let that be enough for me," he was feeling his way along here.

Her insatiable joy and humor had overshadowed every memory, but there had also been her expression as she'd sat behind her brother's desk: an expedition leader overwhelmed by the vast wilderness in every direction. That brief glimpse of sadness as she'd sat alone in the Music Room before he invited her out to the Conservatory concert.

"But that wasn't enough for you. I can see that now, but I didn't before. Or maybe I did but chose to ignore it. So, talk to me, Anne Darlington, and I promise to listen."

"I—" she looked away and brushed her hand on Mephista's muzzle. "I don't know what to talk about. It's…I don't even know what *it* is."

Zack didn't either. But he knew a question that must lay near the core of the matter and it had an answer he definitely wanted to change. It was a Hail Mary play. When the quarterback had no hope of saving the game and no time, he risked everything. Heave the ball high and long, let it loft through the air forever in a clean spiral that seemed to defy gravity, and pray that there was someone able to catch it far down in the endzone.

He took her hand and tugged her gently away from her horse. He led her to the edge of the ridge and guided them to a fallen log overlooking the rolling mountains bathed in the morning sun. Hoping to keep the connection, he didn't release her hand but went for the grand play, the Hail Mary of them all.

"Tell me why you said no."

And as the morning passed and the sun warmed the day, she did. They spoke of her not wanting to be merely Mrs. Zachary Thomas, not Mrs. Second Lady, not even Mrs. First. For the first time, they spoke of her dreams and his. Of the brilliant, vivacious woman unable to find what she wanted and the lonely boy who, in seeking approval of others might one day lead the nation.

"I'm supposed to give you this," he fished into his pocket. Genny had said he would know when to hand it to Anne and though she'd refused to say how he'd know, she'd been right. He did.

"It's a job offer," Anne read it. "Genny is the UNESCO World Heritage Centre's 'Ambassador' to the General Assembly. She is offering me a job as her special assistant in charge of all natural-site applications."

"What do you think?" It sounded like Anne Darlington, and he liked that.

His answer came when she cradled the letter to her chest beneath clasped hands.

This time he was the one to brush the hot tears from her cool cheeks.

"What?"

"I would love to do this. I don't think I knew how much until she and I talked about it for so long…while you were busy tracing my phone call location." She glared up at him, but it worried him less than it might have a few hours ago.

"*I* would never do such a thing to the woman I love," he hooked a thumb toward Harvey. "*He* did it for me."

"The woman you love," she didn't make it a question which he also found deeply encouraging.

"Yes, Anne Darlington. And I seem to recall that you said the same thing about me."

"I remember that too," she read the letter in her hands again, then cradled it back against her chest. She looked out at the horizon for a long time and he let her be.

He too looked out, more than a glance which was all he'd spared the view since they'd arrived. He could see why she loved this spot, had come here seeking answers. Her mother had said that was what Anne did, rode off into the wilds of the estate and always came back so much surer of herself. He could see why.

She belonged here.

He'd like to show her the mountains of Colorado, but he could see them ending up here. His home was no more than a set of trains sprawled across a large basement and memories of a father who was rarely home. Here a family could grow. Here there might be a place for the both of them in some distant future.

"Zachary?" It was the first time she'd used his full name except by accident.

"Yes, Anne?" She still looked out at the land, but he knew that she too was looking far into the future rather than at the rolling forests of the Smoky Mountains.

"When it's time for you to ask your question again, I'll have a different answer for you."

And she was right, it wasn't time yet to ask. Like Genny Matthews' job offer, Zack knew that he'd know when the time was right to do so.

They sat hip to hip on the log, his arm around her waist, and watched the sun chase the shadows over the hills.

Chapter 12

Z*ack's second trip to* the Darlington Farm was as unlike the first as could be. The first time he'd come with fear in his heart and the First Lady's diatribe on idiot men still ringing in his ears.

This time it was the Darlingtons who had extended the invitation and they all had come. Not just he and Daniel with his Alice, but the First Family as well. The Secret Service had done their usual job of securing the property, made easier because the party had remained small.

"We agreed years ago," Mary Annette Darlington had informed him, "that each family who works the estate would have their own Christmas and be with their own families. For Thanksgiving, the Fourth of July and so on, we are all together, but for all of us the Darlington Estate is closed and private for Christmas."

That didn't mean they lacked the capacity to set out a grand spread when the occasion arose. They not only fed the Secret Service agents who had to work the Protection Details in two separate shifts of Christmas dinner. Zack and Anne had also made sure that the families of the men and women who had fought the Italian avalanche with him were invited as well.

The main estate itself was a grand set of buildings. Much like the White House, the lower stories of the old plantation house had been converted into the offices, kitchens, and tourist areas. The family ranged very comfortably throughout the top floor. They filled four of the five bedrooms. Any fantasies he'd had picturing Anne skiing were more than allayed by the magnificent series of photos of her with her horses and their trophies that adorned her room. The age progression of a beautiful girl growing into a stunning woman each in high boots, jodhpurs, helmet, and form-fitting black wool blazer was enough to undo him.

Downstairs, the period furniture had been preserved and the simpler period Christmas decorations had been hung. Not so upstairs. Great swags of holly and spruce were draped about the central sky-lit hall. In the very center stood a tree as grand as the White House's Blue Room Christmas tree. It was decorated with two hundred years of handmade ornaments; some were simple children's work, others were utterly elegant.

"These were Anne's work when she was younger," Mary Annette whispered with obvious pride as she toured him about the tree. Her gesture picked out a cluster of six eggshells. They'd been poked at either end to be emptied and allow a ribbon to be threaded through the middle. The white surfaces had been pen-and-inked with fine geometric patterns in a wide variety of colors. "It's in the Hungarian tradition, not that we can boast anything so exotic in our heritage. The Darlington's are very boringly Anglo-Saxon I fear."

Johnny Darlington, Anne and Daniel's father, had taken him on a tour of the estate. He was gruff at first but slowly warmed up to him as the evening chilled. Zack could soon see just where Anne had inherited her wry sense of the ridiculous from; not from her studiously perfect mother, but from the taciturn farmer who loved the land as much as his daughter did.

The highlight of Christmas Eve was definitely the meal. Actually, it was cooking the meal that was the most fun.

Being a family that had practically founded the American branch of the Italian Slow Food movement, they had a magnificent kitchen in the residence. Much of the day was spent in and out of the expansive room with its long counters of polished granite and multitude of burners and ovens. Beveled glass fronted the cupboards filled with china and crystal. A large pantry extended off one side. The dark hardwood shone with the high polish not from wax but rather from generations of feet crossing and recrossing the surface. The windows looked out over the estate's lands where the food had come from.

The preparations began with Johnny carrying in a large ham clearly stamped "Darlington Farms." But Anne and her mother were definitely the women in charge and the First Lady was soon in the midst of the fray. The three women were wearing aprons and laughing as they worked.

"I can barely barbeque," Zack had confessed when asked.

"I'm shocked," Anne pressed her fingers against her breast. "How did they ever let you into Colorado, never mind make you their governor?"

"I cheated, I was born there. And I never told. It's my dirty little secret."

"Well, it's out now," Anne had dragged him to a counter and pointed at a pile of carrots. "You know how to use a peeler, don't you?"

He had to confess that he did and was soon put to work washing and peeling.

"Sucker," Alice mouthed at him. She was in the kitchen, but had managed to stay on the sidelines as she played with the First Child. Adele Gloria Sebiya Matthews was a year old and about the cutest thing he'd ever seen. It was easy to imagine Alice playing with her own child someday.

Then he glanced at Anne as she and Genny leaned down to consult a recipe that looked as if it had been scribed generations before. Anne with a child, with their child…that too was easy to imagine. Very easy.

Anne's mother must have read his expression and winked at him.

He leaned over to the President who had been relegated to cutting up fresh pumpkin for pumpkin pies, "What is it with Darlington women that they always know what we're thinking?"

"Trust me, Zack, it's not just the Darlington women. I dare you to try and slip something past Genny. I need to warn you, as President to hopefully next President, forget the Russians or the Chinese. The truly inscrutable ones are our women."

"Love them like mad—"

"Absolutely!" Peter agreed.

"—but never understand them."

"Not a chance."

And then Anne looked at him as if she'd just overheard the entire conversation, which was impossible as Daniel was making a walnut flour in the food processor at that moment. Her smile said yes to so many things.

# # #

"Here, this one is for you, Pop," Anne had been chosen as the Darlington's Santa, which included a silly red hat and the duty of parsing out gifts from beneath the tree.

Last night's feast had gone long into the night but Anne had little to contribute. Her awareness of Zack had grown until she'd lost her capacity for words and was content to just listen and enjoy as Genny and her mother had compared notes on handling men. The President and her father had done their best to pretend they couldn't hear the stories that were being laughed about around the whole table.

The two women had also discussed the birth and initial year of the First Daughter, asleep in the cradle beside the First Lady's chair, in such graphic detail that Anne had finally spoken up to forbid that topic.

Her mother, the premier social tactician, had already forbidden politics and farming from the table which had initially left the two men adrift, but they had eventually joined in on other matters.

Zack had been as quiet as she was.

Last night, when she'd finally taken him to her bed, neither of them had found any words. They'd been gentle and loving and it told her that she was only at the very beginning of learning what the future held for them both. When he'd rested his hand upon her bare belly for a long moment, she'd only been able to tuck her head against his chest and nod. Someday. Someday soon. And then their child was going to grow up in a very unique house.

This morning she'd found her voice again, "I have to warn you, Pop," she pointed at the package's label, "this is from my brother, so it must be a tie." Something her father had never worn except at formal dinners.

Instead it was a fine-knit scarf of gold leaves, blue sky, and running horses—hooves raised high in the trademark Tennessee Walker stride. It had been double-knit so that both sides were finished. Alice's handiwork.

"Oh my god, I want one. I'm going to steal yours, Pop. Watch out."

"Not a chance, Melanie Anne Darlington." He wrapped it around his neck and flipped it in a loose knot to make his point.

"No you aren't," Alice said sternly. She plucked another box from under the tree, "You're going to open this instead."

It was a perfect match, except for her initials worked into the sky at one end. She put hers on, kissed Alice, reminded her that she was Anne's number one favorite sister-in-law, and went to hug her father.

He pulled her into his lap, something he hadn't done in years, and pulled her head down to kiss her soundly on the top of it. She snuggled in for just a moment, before sitting up and holding out both of their scarves.

"We match."

"You always were my Johnny's little girl," her mother sighed. "Daniel took after me but like your father, you're happiest when you're out on the land. I kept trying to convince you that running the estate was in your blood, but it isn't."

"No, it's in Daniel's," the President noted. "I promise, I'll give him back in just a few more years. Anne was right, this is where he's supposed to be, but I still need him for a while."

"How didn't I know that?" Anne slid onto the footstool and turned to face her father, resting her elbows on his knees. Her build and coloring, even her accent was from her mother. She'd always thought she was destined to be just like her. "How did I miss that?"

Her father, always a man of few words, reached out to brush a hand down her cheek and tap a finger on her nose as he always used to, "Weren't paying attention, were you? You were always bigger than this place, always thinking outside the box."

"Your cookies," her mother groaned. "I'll never forgive you, Johnny, for getting her started on those cookies."

And Anne realized that's where she'd gotten it from. She'd never thought about it, but could remember her father teaching her how to make cookie boxes with "airholes" in them and a reindeer antler sticking out through one. And it wasn't just the cookies; it was the whispered wry comments, the off-kilter observations, that had only been between them.

Her mother was regaling the room with the trials and tribulations she'd suffered when Anne and her Johnny were collaborating on any number of projects. She and her father were left in a small moment of space. She looked up into his deep blue eyes, the only physical thing she'd inherited from him.

"Love you, Pop."

"You're glowing, honey. All I ever asked for."

"I'm happy. Maybe for the first time since I last rode Mephista to the steeplechase."

"About to get better, honey. Turn around."

And there was Zack. Somehow he'd absconded with her official Santa hat and now sat on the floor at the foot of the tree.

"There are two presents for Queen Anne, one big and one small," he intoned as if announcing something to a royal court. "Which would she like first?"

"Big one, duh, Mr. Vice President!"

"A wise choice, my queen," he winked at her before calling out. "Bring in the big present."

And Alice came in carrying what Anne first thought was a stuffed toy dog—until it squirmed in her arms, released an ear-shattering yip of excitement, and licked Alice's face.

"Eww! No fair. You're not mine, you little terror. Here, sister-in-law, I think this troublemaker must be yours."

Anne held up her hands, "Oh, gimme! Gimme! Gimme!" The puppy had no qualms about transferring to her arms. It nestled happily in her lap and licked Anne's nose. Her—Anne lifted the dog's front legs to check—her fur was one of the softest things Anne had ever felt.

"She's a Sheltie," Zack reached out to scratch the dog's head and received a nipped finger for his troubles. "Big enough to be a real dog and keep up on hikes, small enough travel with you or even to be trained to ride in a saddlebag when you go horsing about the countryside."

Anne poked her nose against the dog's cool one and got a happy tongue loll as a reward. "She's perfect. I'm going to name her Zackie, because she's probably going to be just as much trouble as the man who gave her to me."

"And if you call her Zackie, what are you going to call me?"

"I think that should be obvious, Mr. Vice President." At his groan she waved a hand at the big box she'd tucked around the side of the tree. "That is your *big* present."

"He's going to love this," she whispered into the dog's fur and hugged it tight on her lap. They'd never spoken of it, but he'd known she was a dog person. Maybe he knew about farms. On a working farm a cat wasn't a pet, it was a furry form of rodent control that occasionally condescended to scratch a little girl for petting it. Dogs were what kept a person company. And the White House did have a long tradition of canine residents.

Zack sat cross-legged before the tree. He began methodically unpeeling one of the back flaps of his gift and she sighed.

She scooted down to sit on the living room carpet in front of him, keeping Zackie in her lap. Anne reached out, grabbed a corner of the paper and yanked at it, creating a massive rip.

Everyone leaned forward to see what it was. But she didn't care about them. She just watched the man she'd come to love so easily as her gift registered. It was with almost reverent hands that he peeled back the rest of the paper.

When he looked up at her, it wasn't the man's eyes that looked at her, it was the boy's. But this time they were filled with hope.

"A fresh start. For the whole family. For you, for me, for our children. Maybe not for this scamp," she waved one of the puppy's paws at him.

He looked back down at the train set.

"The train shop—who knew there was such a thing—said it was the very best starter kit. I bought it in N-gauge, one size bigger than the one you had as a child so there could be no borrowing. A true fresh start."

Again he looked at her with his soul bared before her. He pulled her in and kissed her. The puppy barked loudly then licked the bottom of both of their chins from where it was confined between them.

"Okay, maybe I need to rethink the dog gift," Zack muttered as they parted.

"Don't you dare," she hugged the puppy close which made it wriggle with delight.

"You make my small present almost irrelevant, my dear Anne."

"Gimme! Gimme! Gimme!" She repeated her earlier call earning her a laugh from her family and the First Family except for Adele who was happily asleep on the belly of a stuffed bear that was larger than she was.

He reached into his jeans pocket and extracted a square blue-velvet box and opened it. Inside was a simple, yet elegant ring. It had a single emerald the color of the forest set in a twisted band of silver and gold. No chill diamond of ice or frozen hearts. Two precious metals combined to grow together, becoming a luminously green future larger than either of them could imagine.

"I think you've struck her speechless," Alice called from somewhere behind her.

"Yes, there are times that a man can do just that," Genny whispered softly.

Anne heard a sniffle from her mother, but couldn't look away.

Zack remained sitting before her, complete Santa hat in front of the family Christmas tree, holding aloft the incredible gift of his heart.

"You said your answer might be different if I asked again?"

Anne could only nod. It was all so fast, but it wasn't, because it was also so perfect.

"Well?" he whispered to her.

"You have to ask if you want an answer," she whispered back.

"Oh, right." Zack rose to kneeling on one knee and spoke up. "Melanie Anne Darlington, before these good friends and family, will you make me whole for the rest of our days? For everyone knows I am incomplete without you. Please marry me."

"Oh god yes, Mr. Vice President." No need to hold her breath for even an instant to be sure of that. He understood that she couldn't say yes while she'd only been half a person, but neither could she be whole without him.

Once he'd slipped the ring onto her finger, she threw herself at him, knocking him flat on his back among the piles of torn up wrapping paper.

She kissed him under the Christmas tree while everyone else cheered and clapped, and a puppy chased a small blue velvet box across the rug beside them.

About the Author

M. *L. Buchman has* over 40 novels in print. His military romantic suspense books have been named Barnes & Noble and NPR "Top 5 of the Year," nominated for the Reviewer's Choice Award for "Top 10 Romantic Suspense of 2014" by RT Book Reviews, and twice Booklist "Top 10 of the Year" placing two of his titles on their "The 101 Best Romance Novels of the Last 10 Years." In addition to romance, he also writes thrillers, fantasy, and science fiction.

In among his career as a corporate project manager he has: rebuilt and single-handed a fifty-foot sailboat, both flown and jumped out of airplanes, designed and built two houses, and bicycled solo around the world.

He is now making his living as a full-time writer on the Oregon Coast with his beloved wife. He is constantly amazed at what you can do with a degree in Geophysics. You may keep up with his writing by subscribing to his newsletter at www. mlbuchman.com.

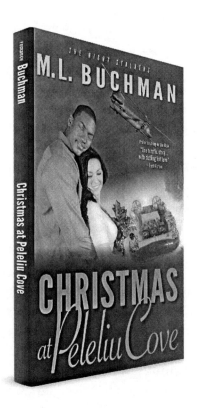

This Christmas you might also enjoy:

Chirstmas at Peleliu Cove
(excerpt)

Striding up the wide steel bow ramp of the LCAC hovercraft, Petty Officer Nika Maier patted the ugly beast on its big black numbers—316—painted on the Navy-gray hull.

"Morning, baby." It was 1800 hours, an hour past sunset in the southern Mediterranean, the start of their day. Ever since the Night Stalkers had come to fly helicopters off their ship, operations had been done in a flipped-clock world of night. Even in their second year aboard, she really wasn't used to sleeping through the day, but that choice was made way above the pay grade of a Navy enlisted woman. Despite the warm December evening, there was a familiar damp air-and-steel chill down in the bowels of the USS *Peleliu* where Landing Craft Air Cushion 316 was typically parked.

"You got a soft spot in you," Chief Petty Officer Sly Stowell's deep voice echoed about the steel cavern that was the sea-level Well Deck of the ship. The *Peleliu's* massive stern ramp was currently raised, blocking out both the sea and the last of the sunset. In the shadows of the worklights she hadn't spotted him. The Craftmaster was perched in the window of the hovercraft's starboard two-story control station, but after four years aboard his craft and four tours in the Navy, she'd lost her the ability to be surprised and simply waved a greeting.

"Only before a mission," she looked up at him. "Other than that..."

"...hard as steel," he finished for her. "In a mood to go kick some ass, Petty Officer Maier?" He offered his ritual start-of-shift greeting.

"Two boots better than one, Chief Stowell," her ritual reply before she climbed up into her Loadmaster's portside tower to prep the hovercraft. Even on days with no mission or exercise planned, they always made sure their craft was completely ready.

Sly dropped down the ladder and headed off to the evening briefing as she started checking over the LCAC—spoken like you were about to throw up—El-Cack! Some part of her warped Lower East Side Jewish sense of humor laughed every single time she heard it...or even thought it. The LCAC was homely as a New York bum, and so powerful that riding in it felt like an outing in the Lord's personal chariot. The juxtaposition got her every time. Probably made her completely sophomoric, but since no one could hear inside her head she figured no harm—no foul.

The portside lookout on Sly Stowell's hovercraft had become Petty Officer Nika Maier's favorite assignment since joining the Navy eight years before. In just another month she'd have been four years on old Lady 316.

Her first tour had been aboard the USS *George H. W. Bush*—then on its own first tour—but a girl could get totally lost in the five-thousand person city that was a newly commissioned aircraft carrier. The largest ship afloat in any navy, and still the crowd was worse than Times Square on New Year's Eve. She'd been a "red"—a red-vested serviceperson—in charge of loading and securing aircraft weapons and munitions systems. She was no aviator, but eventually grew sick of watching others burn into the sky on the hottest rides while she stood on the deck, ate exhaust fumes, and wished she was someone else.

For a brief time, a very brief time, the length of a two-week training run, she'd switched over to a Cyclone-class patrol boat without an aircraft in sight—not even a helipad. The hundred-and-eighty foot boat got in close to the action, mostly on security patrols for bigger ships. She'd enjoyed that. And the weapon systems were exceptional—there were six major weapon systems on a boat commonly crewed by just thirty men and women.

But that was the catch. On the USS *Firebolt*, a girl *couldn't* get lost. With such a small crew, the pickings were painfully thin for friendships, never mind any other thoughts. And the *Firebolt's* grapevine news network offered no privacy at all—you couldn't switch from drinking ice tea to lemonade at lunch without raising comments and questions. Good people, just way too far into your life.

Nika's Loadmaster checklist on the LCAC was short until they had a load. It was still fifteen minutes to start of shift, so she grabbed Jerome's checklist and began the mechanical inspection. She was the only one other than Sly who had cross-trained in all five of the crew positions; but it required constant practice to keep her skills fresh. Step one: Perimeter inspection. She headed down the bow ramp and began working her way along the spray skirt looking for untoward damage. The vague slit of light coming in over the *Peleliu's* rear ramp was no help at all, but the big worklights shone down. She pulled a flashlight out of her thigh pocket to double-check in the shadows cast by the overheads.

This, her third ship—three hundred feet shorter and half the personnel of the super carrier—landed right in the sweet spot. The USS *Peleliu* had serviced a Marine Expeditionary Unit for thirty-five years. Cobra helicopters and Harrier jets up on the flattop deck. Beneath that and the Hanger Deck were several decks carrying fifteen hundred gung-ho Marines and a third that many Navy to run the eight-hundred foot ship.

Even though Nika had liked the size, she'd still felt disconnected. Most of her second tour had gone by and she'd been doubting the point of re-upping for a third.

Then, four years ago, Sly had introduced her to heaven. She patted her baby-girl 316 again as she inspected the rear ramp gasket seal. She remembered the day with crystal clarity—

It had been midday and the Indian Ocean heat had dehydrated her to the point of weaving, weighed down by her bright red fire-resistant gear. She'd just left the Flight Deck after double-checking the Zuni missile control connections on yet another SuperCobra helicopter when Chief Petty Officer Sly Stowell had pulled her aside. Everyone knew Sly, he was just one of *those* guys. Super competent. There were days it seemed the *Peleliu* would sink without him aboard. Other times people said that they didn't need a command structure as long as Sly was around.

"You look bored as hammered shit, Maier," were the first words he'd ever spoken directly to her. She hadn't realized that he even knew her name.

Sometimes you answered honesty with honesty.

"Damn straight, Chief. If I never have to load another Hydra 70 missile tube, I'll die a happy woman."

"Good, come with me," and he'd walked away from her.

At a loss for what else to do, she'd grabbed a water bottle and staggered after him.

He'd led her down past the personnel decks. Even below the on-board Garage Decks filled with tanks, Humvees, and a dozen different land and amphibious vehicles. They were packed in so tightly that drivers used the roof hatches to get in and out of them once they were parked because they were jammed into the ship's lower holds door to door.

He led her down to the Well Deck. She hadn't been down here but once or twice since her on-boarding orientation tour two years before. The air had been oddly fresher than up on the exposed burning plain of the Flight Deck, and thanks be to the Lord our God.

Right at sea-level, the *Peleliu* sported a massive stern gate. When lowered into the water it formed an angled steel beach, opening the Well Deck directly to the sea. A variety of landing craft could be parked there.

"Meet my baby," Sly had sounded like a proud papa despite being from North Carolina rather than a good Jewish family. Or even a bad one like hers.

It was an LCAC, about the ugliest sea craft ever built. No surprise that they named the craft so that it sounded like a cat choking up a hairball. Worse, its only name was the black numbers painted as tall as Nika's torso. Aircraft, ships, even sailboats had names; El-Cacks didn't even rate that.

A Landing Craft Air Cushion was a ninety-foot-long by fifty-foot-wide rectangular platform with four jet engines down the sides—combined, they packed the same power as a Boeing 737 airliner. She sported two huge fans at the stern and two more that drove air underneath her big rubber skirt. There was a two-story control station at the starboard front corner for three people and a smaller tower for some loner to port. After the mayhem of the Flight Deck, that isolated tower had looked attractive.

At the base of either tower was a narrow cabin for a total of thirty troops. Behind them, on each side, were two big gas turbine jet engines and then the two massive rear fans. Down the center was the broad deck that could hold an M1A1 Abrams Main Battle Tank or a dozen armored Humvees parked in three tight lanes.

She finished rounding the craft doing her start of day inspection and looked up at it. Four years later, she still liked the look of it. Every now and then someone would tease her about being the "fair maiden locked in a tower." They didn't understand that from up there she could watch the world go by and not have to worry that her every thought conformed to some unwritten set of her mother's rules. Given the choice, she'd lock the door so that they could never drag her away.

Even on that first day aboard four years ago, she'd felt a strange affinity for the poor beast of a machine. Neither boat nor aircraft, the hovercraft lay there on the Well Deck like a stuck pig with her rubber skirt deflated and the front and rear ramps laying open on the rough wood of the presently dry Well Deck. The LCAC looked like someone had slashed open either end of a giant steel shoebox and pushed the end flaps down.

Nika had left the Flight Deck in broad daylight and fresh sea air—liberally laced with the kerosene bite of fresh-burned Jet-A fuel and echoing with the roar of turboshaft engines. The bowels of the ship were dark and quiet except for the beat of the sea against the outside of the hull and the low thrum of the big steam turbines directly below—more felt through the heels of her boots than heard. With the *Peleliu's* stern gate up, only a narrow slice of light entered above the gate. Big worklights did little to chase away the shadowed cave that was the Well Deck. It was like a man-cave on steroids—without the bar and big-screen television.

"Ain't she a beauty?" Sly had asked in his lazy Southern drawl, which echoed about the vast compartment like a whisper in Temple Emanu-el, the massive synagogue that her mother always dragged her to for the high holidays. As if showing up ten times a year somehow made them Upper East Side New York Jews rather than the last of the Lower East Side holdouts against the encroaching Chinatown. Encroaching, hell. The Chinese had overrun the old Jewish neighborhood and most of Little Italy…but the Maiers would not be nudged loose from their appointed place in the world.

Thankfully Sly didn't wait for her to answer.

"She needs a crew of five to fly and I just lost my portside spotter and Loadmaster," he aimed a nod up at the slim one-person tower that she'd liked on first sight. "Something about falling in love with an accountant, wants kids. You want kids, Maier?"

"Not yet, Chief. Haven't found a man worth having them with."

"Good. You already have your boatswain's rating. Welcome aboard."

And just that simply she'd been transferred to the LCAC crew—so fast that Sly might have sent in the paperwork before she'd ever descended the ladders and ramps to view her new posting. Her new world. The first part of her job was as weapons specialist to their pair of M2 .50 cal machine guns. Bit of a letdown from Harrier jets' and SuperCobra helicopters' vast array of heavy armament, but for the first time in her service, one of the machine guns was exclusively hers to control.

Also, he'd tempted her with the word "fly," because that's what an LCAC did—mere feet above the water but it flew.

Then Chief Stowell had followed up rapidly with Loadmaster training, assistant navigator, understudy engineer, and for her fourth tour he'd offered to start her on Craftmaster training, his own gig.

She'd re-upped.

And Sly was of course as good as his word, one of the main reasons she'd stuck with him for four years now. Men who weren't trying to sell a girl something were an unusual commodity in her experience, in or out of the service. Sly didn't sell anything.

He actually believed. He was a lifer and was slowly convincing her that was a good thing. For lack of any clearer plan, she was starting to buy in.

Then right after she'd re-upped, the Marines had abandoned the *Peleliu* and tossed her toward the scrap heap. The Navy crew that ran her had gone into a deep tailspin of ugly funk. The band would be split up and scattered across the Navy. All of the newer personnel were indeed gone within days of the Marines' departure until under a quarter of her normal Navy crew remained. All of them who remained were old hands, not one below a rank of Petty Officer Second Class. Everyone assumed it was to oversee the decommissioning.

"Weirdest thing I've ever seen," Sly had mused quietly when the others had shipped out. "This is about the finest crew I've ever seen left aboard a doomed boat." They didn't have to wait long to find out why.

Just a few days later, in the dark of a long night the Night Stalkers of the US Army's 160th Special Operation Aviation Regiment 5th Battalion D Company had whispered aboard. With a full load, the *Peleliu* could carry thirty aircraft, the Night Stalkers brought seven.

But *whispered* was the operative word. Most of the 5D's helos were stealth-rigged, which Nika hadn't known existed outside of the raid on bin Laden's compound.

Instead of fifteen hundred Marines, the aging *Peleliu* shipped aboard the Night Stalkers 5D, six Delta operators, and thirty Special Operations grunts from the 75th Rangers. Since that night, the laughably small team had led them from crisis to crisis throughout Africa and the Middle East in a whirlwind which still wasn't showing any sign of easing. She'd seen more action in the eighteen months since their arrival than in her first six years in the Navy combined.

Her decision to join Sly's team—of which she was still the newest member even after four years—had been the best of her life. A close second had been dodging Mom's attempt to marry her off to Brian, *soon to be Doctor, honey,* Goldman. She'd have been better off with his younger brother Richie, a sweet geek, rather than that arrogant son of a bitch. Richie had eventually gone military and she'd lost track of him, not that it really mattered. Out of a million active soldiers in the US Armed Services she hadn't run into him or any other person she'd known back in the neighborhood—definitely her idea of good fortune.

Still no sign of Sly returning from the evening briefing by the time the other three of the LCAC crew arrived from "breakfast" just as the last of the sunset's glow disappeared above the stern gate. She didn't mention that she'd already done all three of their inspections; just enjoyed that they didn't find a single thing to do on their rounds. They were soon gathered in a line at the head of the bow ramp. Nothing happened.

"Five gets you a hundred we're on our butts again today," Tom Trambley, the craft's Navigator, grumbled.

"Maybe if you weren't such a shrimp, they wouldn't underestimate us so much and we'd draw more missions," Dave Newcomb, the craft's Engineer, looked down at his best friend. At six foot four of gangly North Dakotan, Dave was the tallest member of their crew, and the only one who could refer to Tom's six-three as short. Nika's five-six still left her a head shorter than any of them.

Jerome Walker, the Deck Mechanic and Assistant Loadmaster, typically didn't say a word.

"Maybe if you were shorter," Tom glared up at Dave, "you wouldn't make us look so damn ridiculous. Jerome, you're gonna have to cut us a hole in the control cabin roof just for Dave's swollen ego. Course he spent all that height growing his head, means his pecker is the size of a bean."

"You'd know," Nika was feeling good so she joined in the fray. The Chief's evening mission briefing was running too long for an exercise.

Jerome's snort of laughter was as much as he ever said unless something was broken or some grunt didn't park their vehicle exactly as he directed—he was the LCAC's other Loadmaster. When that happened his Georgia came out thick and biting. No Marine or Ranger made that mistake again if they could help it.

A clatter of steps on the ramp down from the Garage Deck cut off Tom's sputtering response. They all recognized Sly's confident stride, but there were more people behind him; a guaranteed conversation stopper.

Yep! Nika kept the thought to herself about getting the last word. *Timing was everything.*

Tom was such an easy target that teasing him wasn't really fair, not that it stopped her of course. He was the only one of them other than Sly who sported a wedding ring. He had a wife and kid back home and almost never shut up about them—proud dad didn't begin to cover it. Way too easy a target.

Sly had hooked up with the ship's Chief Steward last Christmas; hooked up permanently right down to the ring and a white wedding ashore with family and the whole nine yards. Nika had been invited and had worn her formal dinner-dress whites—with the slacks option. She didn't even own the skirt option for her dress whites and absolutely not a damned gown. She'd sworn off dresses as soon as she'd grown old enough to face down her mother. And a wedding dress? Never gonna happen, even if Gail now-Stowell had looked completely amazing in hers.

"Make 'er ready," Sly's call echoed down the ramp before he made the last turn into view at the head of the Well Deck. It was the same words he used to start every live mission. A training exercise started, "Let's go prove we still know how."

"Way ahead of you, Chief," Nika replied as he swung into view at a quick stride. Then she couldn't resist, "Had it all inspected and prepped before any of these jokers even showed up."

"What?" Tom exclaimed and Dave just looked bummed. Jerome nodded as if to say, "Of course you did."

She heard the distant sound of several small engines coughing to life up in the garages and her pulse picked up its pace. "What kind of heat are we packing tonight?" She and Jerome had to make sure that any vehicles were positioned so that the LCAC's loading was properly balanced and she'd fly true.

"Lots of little heat, Petty Officer Maier," a deep voice wrapped in a soft Southern deeper and richer than Sly's called out from the head of the loading ramp. "Fast and dirty heat. And a pair of RSOVs just in case." Ranger Spec Ops Vehicles—they absolutely confirmed there was action tonight.

Nika glanced up the ramp to see Lieutenant Clint Barstowe arrive close behind Sly. The commander of the 75th Rangers platoon was a big man, and loaded for bear. Combat uniform, armored vest, and enough magazines for his rifle to take out an entire platoon of bad guys himself. He looked incredible. Not overly handsome, just damned good looking. Strong shoulders on a powerful frame. But mostly he radiated power—dark and dangerous. It wasn't that you didn't want to meet him in a trashy alley; even in broad daylight you'd best pray he was on your side.

His helmet was snagged on his belt, hooked over the butt of his knife. His service piece holstered on the other hip and a rifle over his shoulder.

Then he totally spoiled the pretty picture by wearing a red Santa hat complete with white fur trim and pom-pom perched atop his Ranger-short black hair.

# # #

"Need to grow a white beard if you're planning to live up to that hat, Lieutenant. Besides, you're a little early there. And aren't you from Arkansas? Do they even have Christmas that far south?"

Clint grinned at the heckler in surprise. Maier was always teasing people, but it was the first time she'd aimed a jibe at him in the eighteen months he'd been aboard.

"You snickering at my festive fedora, Petty Officer Nika Maier? Thanksgiving is a week gone; it's December now. Where's your Christmas spirit, Petty Officer?"

"I'm Jewish, Lieutenant. And we're in the Southern Mediterranean where it's seventy-eight Fahrenheit."

"And you're using that as an excuse *not* to be merry?"

"As I said, sir, Jewish. Against our religion to be merry because we don't need an excuse to feel someone is out to get us—we already know they are. Besides, that's not a fedora without a brim and an indented crown." She picked up a three-foot steel pry bar used for tightening the vehicle tie-down chains and waved it at him, revealing a surprising strength in her slender frame. "Be glad to fix the latter problem for you," her cheerful tone completely belied her prior declaration regarding merriness.

"And you never had a Christmas tree? I can only pity the poor, neglected child."

"Might have had a Hanukkah bush, sir. Might have had pretty lights on it. Maybe even presents that were opened on December 25th. But I promise, I wasn't merry about it."

Damn but he liked her. Nika Maier had sass and a slow smile that was hard to tease out, but it was definitely worth the effort. And she always gave a hundred percent just like a Ranger and it was easy to respect that, even if she was a Navy swabbie. More Navy swabbies looked like her and he just might change branches of the service.

"My beard comes in as black as my hair, ma'am. Black as my mama's." Lena Barstowe was still acclaimed as a beautiful woman even in her fifties. And able to stare down the entire board of the Little Rock hospital she ran if she didn't like one of their decisions.

"A mama's boy. I should have known."

"Not the way you mean it, but yes. Hundred percent! Hoo-ah!"

She'd come up the hard way, nurse to senior administrator— doing a whole lot to respect. Raising he and his little sister on her own, she'd been both warm and strict. And he'd do anything to protect them both.

"So you're a lump of coal Santa. Wouldn't want to find you in my stocking; could ruin a whole Hanukkah Bush day. And *Ma'am?* Do I look like a ma'am?"

Nika Maier looked like a lot of good things he wouldn't mind finding in stockings and a Ms. Claus mini-dress—an image he decided to keep to himself, especially because she hadn't set aside that steel bar yet. Clint went for a different conversation though the image didn't exactly fade away.

"Can't say I much like sleighs either. Especially y'alls air cart," he did his best to make the last a dismissive sneer, as beneath a gentleman soldier of Little Rock.

Maier brandished her pry bar again, proving the correctness of his earlier decision on keeping certain things to himself. "You take that back, Army. Nobody insults our little girl 316 and gets away with it."

Available at fine retailers everywhere
More information at:
www.mlbuchman.com

Other works by M. L. Buchman:

The Night Stalkers
The Night Is Mine
I Own the Dawn
Daniel's Christmas
Wait Until Dark
Frank's Independence Day
Peter's Christmas
Take Over at Midnight
Light Up the Night
Christmas at Steel Beach
Bring On the Dusk
Target of the Heart
Target Lock on Love
Christmas at Peleliu Cove
Zachary's Christmas

Firehawks
Pure Heat
Wildfire at Dawn
Full Blaze
Wildfire at Larch Creek
Wildfire on the Skagit
Hot Point

Delta Force
Target Engaged

Angelo's Hearth
Where Dreams are Born
Where Dreams Reside
Maria's Christmas Table
Where Dreams Unfold
Where Dreams Are Written

Dieties Anonymous
Cookbook from Hell: Reheated
Saviors 101

Thrillers
Swap Out!
One Chef!
Two Chef!

SF/F Titles
Nara
Monk's Maze

CPSIA information can be obtained at www.ICGtesting.com
Printed in the USA
LVOW09s0020190116

471173LV00003B/612/P